The Lord and the Cat's Meow

A Regency Romance

By

GL Robinson

Cover art: **Henriëtte Ronner-Knip,** 1821–1909

As always, in loving memory of my sister Francine.

For my granddaughter Nina, and animal lovers everywhere.

With thanks to Thomas E. Burch for his patient technical help.

And to my Beta readers, who always tell me what they think.

©GL Robinson 2021. All Rights Reserved

For a FREE short story, please go to the author's website:

https://romancenovelsbyglrobinson.com

Contents

Chapter One 1
Chapter Two 11
Chapter Three 15
Chapter Four 29
Chapter Five 33
Chapter Six 38
Chapter Seven 45
Chapter Eight 51
Chapter Nine 58
Chapter Ten 64
Chapter Eleven 70
Chapter Twelve 79
Chapter Thirteen 85
Chapter Fourteen 92
Chapter Fifteen 100
Chapter Sixteen 107
Chapter Seventeen 113
Chapter Eighteen 119
Chapter Nineteen 125
Chapter Twenty 129
Chapter Twenty-One 136
Chapter Twenty-Two 142
Chapter Twenty-Three 150
Chapter Twenty-Four 158
Chapter Twenty-Five 165
Chapter Twenty-Six 171

Chapter Twenty-Seven	180
Chapter Twenty-Eight	185
Chapter Twenty-Nine	189
Chapter Thirty	194
Chapter Thirty-One	201
Chapter Thirty-Two	208
Chapter Thirty-Three	217
About the Author	227

Chapter One

Lord Elliott Devin stood in front of the ornate gold mirror above the fireplace, and gave his elaborately arranged neckcloth a slight twitch.

"These new neckcloths they sent me just don't sit right. The linen is too fine, I fancy. They collapse the minute after you put them on. Oh well, it'll have to do. I don't want to be late."

"My dear fellow," replied his friend Marius Hingston from where he sat in a comfortable chair with a dark bottle and an empty glass next to him, "it's gone ten and the invitation was for nine. We're already late, and you know it. You're the very devil to keep on time for anything."

He stretched his legs before him, as if prepared to stay where he was even longer. Marius was a devil-may-care fellow, very fond of gambling, and indulging his passion, a frequenter of places most members of the *ton* would avoid. In the sluices of Tothill Fields he'd been known to bet on a race between two rats for a piece of cheese, two cockroaches running up a wall, or how many spiders a new-found acquaintance could eat before he could finish a mug of ale. In this way he'd made many interesting friends.

"Oh, an hour doesn't count as late, Marius," said Lord Devin, as they both moved into the hall. He allowed the butler to place his evening cloak over his shoulders, before drawing on his gloves and taking his hat and cane. "It's just long enough for everyone to become bored with the guests who've already arrived and therefore greet one with real pleasure. Just like you, my friend. I kept you kicking your heels all this time and, admit it, when I finally came downstairs, you were so glad to see me you didn't give me the tongue lashing I undoubtedly deserved."

Marius had passed the time very agreeably betting his right hand against his left on the roll of the dice he always carried in his pocket, with a bottle of his lordship's best port at his elbow. "I know your ways, Elliott," he replied. "I don't know why I bother showing up on time."

"Don't try to gammon me! I am perfectly aware Minton gives you that port you like so much. I believe you arrive early on purpose."

His friend laughed. "There's something in that," he agreed. "It *is* damn fine port!"

And the pair walked companionably the quarter mile to Lady March's London home, where her first ball of the season was being held.

They were nearly two hours late by the time they mounted the carpeted front steps to the elegant townhouse and were announced into the ballroom. But Lord Devin was right. They were greeted with pleasure and real warmth. Of course, it would have been a rare hostess who wasn't pleased to have two of the most eligible bachelors in London at her ball, no matter how late they might be. Lord Devin was a particular favorite. His face and figure were handsome, his address was excellent, and he was always willing to dance with any wallflower a hostess might thrust upon him. It was true he had in this way raised hopes in many a virginal bosom, only to dash them again when, with the gentle charm for which he was famed, he kissed their hand after the one dance and bid them a good evening.

Tonight, however, Lord Devin had a quarry. In his languid way he was seeking out a tall, black-haired lovely he had espied a few nights before. He hadn't seen her previously; she must be a newcomer to the London salons. She had been leaving a rout to which he had arrived even later than usual. He had made a few quiet enquiries and knew now that she was the niece of the well-known socialite Lady Salisbury. She had been on a tour abroad after finishing school, and her aunt had undertaken to bring her out. He saw her now, her height and dark beauty making her visible across the room. He made his way to her side by degrees, stopping for a quiet word here, a shake of the hand there, until he stood before Lady Salisbury and her niece.

"Your ladyship," he bowed. "May I crave an introduction to the vision of loveliness who stands by your side. Even had I not been reliably informed she is your niece, I could have guessed her as a close relative of yours by the remarkable degree of beauty you both share."

Lady Salisbury tapped his arm sharply with her fan. "Don't try your flummery on me, young man! It is only because you are always so unreasonably late that you were not introduced the other day."

"Was I unreasonably late? How careless of me! You see before you a man sunk in a deep despair from which only you can rescue him!" His words were belied by the smile in his eye.

Her ladyship was no more proof against his charm than any other woman. She turned to her niece.

"Hermione, my dear, allow me to present to you Lord Elliott Devin. Under his lazy exterior he is a shocking flirt and reprobate whom I know you have enough sense to put in his place."

And, turning to Elliott, she said, "My niece, Hermione Underwood, my brother's daughter. She lost her mother some years ago, and he has entrusted me with introducing her to society."

Hermione was tall enough that she needed only to raise her eyes to look him straight in the face. She did that now. She had a glorious mane of dark hair and unusual green-brown eyes. Her nose was straight and her lips a perfect bow. She held his gaze calmly for a second then held out her hand. "Lord Devin, delighted," she murmured.

Elliott kissed the proffered hand without taking his eyes from hers. "As am I, my dear Miss Underwood," he said. "How is it that Lady March's ballroom, with which I have been familiar for some years now, suddenly resembles a heavenly paradise with you chief amongst its angels?"

Hermione raised her eyebrows but smiled. "I understand what my aunt means. I can see I shall have to be on my guard."

"Quite unnecessary, I assure you," he smiled back. "Anyone will tell you I am the most harmless of creatures.

But you are not dancing? How can this be? Are the men of London even more than usually obtuse? I would expect to see a line of suitors reaching around the room."

"My niece has danced every dance and is only catching her breath," said Lady Salisbury. "If you look at her card, you will see she is taken for every one. Who is it next, my child?"

Hermione examined her dance card. "Edward Ainsworth. And the next dance is a waltz."

"Teddy Ainsworth?" Lord Devin took her card, and reaching inside his coat, produced a pencil with which he crossed through the name and substituted his own. "There," he said, "that's Teddy dealt with. Come, Miss Underwood, the musicians are about to strike up."

Protesting only mildly, she allowed herself to be led towards the dance floor. On the way there, they met Edward Ainsworth coming to claim his partner.

"I say, Devin," he protested, "what are you…"

"Sorry Teddy," said Elliott. "Force Majeure. Miss Underwood is dancing with me."

"By God, you'll meet me for this!" exclaimed the other man, highly annoyed.

"Any time you like," grinned his lordship. "Name the day. Just don't make it too early in the morning. These dawn confrontations are too much. I need my repose. But for the moment, excuse us. The waltz is beginning."

And the affronted would-be dance partner ground his teeth as the prettiest girl in the room willingly went into the arms of his usurper, who was not only taller and more broad-shouldered than he, but also, as everyone was aware and in spite of his lazy ways, the best fencer and shot in town. Ainsworth would never actually call Devin out, and they both knew it.

He wandered disconsolately into the cardroom and to his surprise, for he was generally a mediocre player, proceeded to win a good deal of money. By the end of the evening, he considered Devin had done him a favor. His winnings were more than fair exchange for a dance, even with a dark-haired beauty, and he went home rejoicing.

If Elliott did not go home rejoicing it was not because he had not enjoyed himself at the ball, but because any excessive emotion was anathema to him. He rarely admitted to anything approaching enthusiasm. His habitual demeanor was a languid insouciance. In fact, he had been much taken with Miss Underwood. He found her unruffled demeanor alluring. It would be exciting to find the passion under that calm exterior.

Over the next weeks he amused himself by trying to provoke her with increasingly scandalous remarks and behavior. A faint color would rise to her cheeks, but she would look up at him directly and calmly. He wondered how far he would need to go before she was genuinely shocked. Quite far, it seemed.

"It's like dancing with an angel," he had said to her at one point while they were waltzing. "You are so light on your feet. But a warm-blooded one. I can see your heart beating." As he spoke he looked towards her white bosom, which was rising and falling delightfully with the exertion of the dance. She had skin so white it was almost transparent.

She knew perfectly well where his glance had fallen and a normal maidenly reaction would have been a violent blush. Her color did heighten, but her look, when she lifted her eyes to his face, was cool.

"Oh, Lord Devin," she said calmly, "don't be misled by my heart. It knows quite well how to behave."

After their dance he relinquished her to another partner, saying he would be back to take her into supper. If he had expected she would glance in his direction or smile at him across the room, he was disappointed. She danced every set until supper with a different cavalier and seemed to enjoy them all equally. When he appeared to take her in, she looked a little puzzled for a moment and then said, with a little laugh, "Oh yes, you are to accompany me to supper. I had forgot."

He didn't believe her but gave her full marks for composure.

The next day, he sent a posy of violent pink dianthus with the note: *I dare you to wear these close to that well-behaved heart.*

The following evening she was at a musical soirée to which he had also been invited, but had initially refused because that was his least favorite form of entertainment. The flimsy spindle-back chairs one was forced to sit on were a torture to someone of his height; the warbling of a soprano with a bosom like a shelf interested him not at all, and there were too many eagle-eyed matrons watching for him to attempt even the mildest flirtation with a pretty girl.

However, on this occasion he sent a note to say he was unexpectedly free, in the certainty the hostess would welcome him with open arms. She did. So, arriving only an hour late, he was treated to the sight of Miss Underwood wearing the bright pink flowers pinned to the bodice of her white gown. She had clearly not only accepted the dare, but gone one better, for she had placed a small bunch of silk flowers of the same color in her dark hair. She looked glorious.

The intermission had just begun and the music lovers were jostling to the table of lemonade, wine-cup and dreary little biscuits, another reason for his dislike of such events. One couldn't even get anything decent to eat or drink. But he went at once to the table, arriving before everyone else, and was in front of his quarry with a glass of the watery lemonade and a plate of biscuits before any of the other attendant swains had a chance.

"Lord Devin!" she exclaimed. "I should be in admiration of your obtaining these refreshments so quickly, but as I happen to know you arrived only just before the intermission and walked right past the table, I refuse to be impressed."

"I, on the other hand, dear lady," he replied with perfect sangfroid, "am very impressed you noticed my arrival. Can it be you were looking for me and not paying attention to the singer?"

She blushed slightly and protested such an unfair accusation.

"May I congratulate you, Miss Underwood," Elliott continued, "on your discernment in the matter of the flowers in your hair. There are not many who would be so bold as to wear that startling shade of pink. Nor carry it off with such élan. It is unforgettable."

She didn't allow him to forget it. She must have visited her *modiste*, for over the next few weeks she appeared in a gown that same shade of shocking pink. All but those determined to dislike her because she made them look insipid agreed that while they themselves would not wear such a color, it really became her very well. It amused Elliott when he heard her described as having unusual but perfect taste.

Over the next few weeks, anyone who knew him would have said that Lord Devin's attentions to Miss Underwood were becoming marked. Since he never did anything other than in his usual languid fashion, those who knew him less well would have noticed nothing. But a few of the older matrons nodded wisely and said he had met his match at last.

Miss Underwood gave no sign of pleasure at being singled out by him. She went smilingly about her business, and appeared to derive as much pleasure from dancing with a newly arrived nobody as with him. She greeted him warmly when he came to her, but never sought him out. His pride was touched. Once or twice he found himself arriving almost on time at events because he wanted to be amongst the first to sign her dance card or obtain a seat close to her. It was then he knew this flirtation was in danger of becoming something more. He asked himself if that was what he really intended. She was the best-looking woman in London, and her real or assumed lack of interest in him intrigued him. So yes, perhaps it was.

Chapter Two

"Stop that immediately!" Wilhelmina Chatterton, known to her friends as Nina, all five feet three inches of her, stood squarely in front of the drayman. "How dare you beat that poor horse! Anyone can see his right hind hoof is giving him trouble. He can hardly walk on it. If he's not moving forward willingly, that is the reason. Whipping him will not improve the situation. If you make him pull the cart further he may collapse altogether."

Then, when the drayman ignored her entirely and lifted his whip again she cried, "Stop it, you brute! Stop it, I say!"

The person thus addressed stopped and stared at this firebrand of a woman. In so doing, he slackened his hold on the whip he was brandishing just long enough for her to seize it from his hand and lay it about his own shoulders. Since these were covered in the thick piece of leather that protected his back when he hoisted up the barrels of beer, it's doubtful he felt anything other than wounded pride at being attacked by a woman half his size. But passers-by were already gathering to watch the fun.

"'Ere!" he bellowed, "Wot yer fink yer doin'? Lay orf! Gimme back that whip."

He attempted to retrieve it, but she nimbly stepped away and put the whip behind her back. Short of manhandling her, which he hesitated to do, especially now that a crowd had gathered, he had no way of getting it back. Her clothing was nondescript and somewhat worn, but from her speech he could tell she was a lady, and besides, the martial light in her eye gave him pause.

"Look 'ere," he said, blustering. "I just got this 'orse from Lord Devin. Cost me a packet and 'e's bin nuffin but trouble."

"I'm not surprised. Only a fool would have bought a horse in this condition. It's quite obvious he has a serious problem with that hoof. Besides, he's not a drayhorse! Anyone can see that! But I can solve your problems for you. I will purchase him. How much do you want?"

The drayman did a rapid calculation. She didn't look very flush in the pocket, but she was a lady and they always had money.

"Well, lookee 'ere, now. I needs payin' for me trouble. They said when I bought 'im that all 'e needed was a new shoe. But 'e's made me late an' I've been twice the time doin' me rounds. Besides, if I sells 'im to you, 'ow am I s'pposed to get 'ome? But I'm thinkin' fifty guineas should cover me costs and me aggravation."

The crowd drew in a collective breath. Fifty guineas! It was a fortune! Surely the lady wouldn't give that much for an old horse?"

She wouldn't.

"Come now, my man, you shouldn't drink so much of what you deliver!" She laughed. The onlookers laughed with her. "I'll give you twenty pounds. Not a penny more. That's far more than you paid for him, I'll warrant. You said yourself he had a problem with his hoof."

The lady proceeded to open her reticule and produce a banknote. The crowd held its breath again.

The drayman said indignantly, "I ain't 'ad a drop, as God's me witness!" Then, not wanting to impugn his manhood by giving up without a fight, "Twenty pounds? Where d'yer fink I'm goin' to get another 'orse for that price?"

"I doubt you paid more than ten guineas for this poor thing. But I don't recommend your going back to Lord… Lord Devin, was it? I'll be talking to him, you may be sure. Selling a horse like this and allowing him to be used in this condition, why it's deliberate cruelty! You and he must both know there's a law against it. I should call a constable."

At the mention of the constable, the fight went out of the drayman. "All right, then, 'and it over." He made as if to take the money.

"Not so fast." The lady put the note back into her reticule and from it withdrew a small tool. "You will use this to straighten the nails and remove the shoe from the hind hoof. Slowly and gently, mind! Then we will need to wrap the hoof. With what, I wonder? Hmm… Just a moment." Turning to the crowd, she said loudly, "Is any gentleman here willing to sell me his gloves, please? Preferably leather ones. I want to put them over the poor animal's hoof. I would use my own, but my hand is too small. I'm prepared to pay ten shillings, even if they're well worn."

Since this was the price of a new pair of gloves, Miss Chatterton had immediate takers. She chose the largest and thickest of the gloves offered and turned them inside out, leaving the fingers folded inwards. She handed them to the drayman.

"Put these on the hoof one on top of the other so the injured part is resting on the padding of the fingers, then tie it securely round the hock. You must have string somewhere on your cart."

Grumbling that he had better things to do than put gloves on a horse's hoof, the drayman nevertheless did as he was bid. Soon the poor animal was able to put his foot down, and when Miss Chatterton took his reins and urged him forward he came readily enough. She paid the man the agreed sum, and advising him not to be fool enough to buy any more injured horses, she was ready to leave. But she stopped.

"What's his name?" she asked over her shoulder.

"Champion," came the answer. "Which he ain't, not by a long chalk. You see if I buys another animal from Lord Devin's stables, not on yer life!"

Chapter Three

Minton, the butler at Devin House, was astonished at 11 o'clock the following morning when, answering a loud knock on the front door, he found himself facing a petite young lady with a very firm chin.

"I wish to see Lord Devin," she announced and not waiting to be invited in, stepped boldly into the foyer.

"Yes, er... Miss..."

"Miss Chatterton. Wilhelmina Chatterton."

"Please step this way, Miss Chatterton," said Minton, regaining his composure. "If you would be so good as to wait in the drawing room, I shall see if his lordship is available."

"Do, and please tell Lord Devin I'm in a hurry. I have a meeting to attend."

"... er, yes, Miss," said the unhappy butler, wondering how he would ever be able to convey such a message to his master who might still be sleeping and would certainly not appreciate any visitor at all at this time in the morning, much less one who seemed to think he would hurry to see her. He decided to get Thompson, his lordship's valet, to perform the office. He was the least likely in the whole household to be told to go to the devil.

In the event, though still in his bed, Lord Devin was awake and was consuming a cup of tea when the valet opened the bedroom door to Minton's discreet knock and received the message that a Miss Chatterton was desirous of speaking with his lordship. She had mentioned she was in a hurry.

"A Miss Chatterton?" repeated Elliott when Thompson conveyed the intelligence. "Do I know her?"

Thompson conferred with the butler, still outside the door.

"No, he doesn't believe so, sir."

"Is she a lady?" The valet was carrying this question to the waiting butler, when Elliott suddenly laughed and said "Oh, for God's sake, tell Minton to come in. It won't be the first time he's seen me in my nightshirt! And I want to hear more about this Miss Chatterton who's in a hurry."

When Minton came silently into the room, his lordship looked at him over the top of his teacup and said, "Well, is she a lady, and more importantly, is she pretty?"

"She is most certainly a lady, my lord," answered the butler solemnly, "and as to whether she is pretty, I think I may say that while she is not a beauty, she is attractive in a …." he sought the word, "… in a somewhat unusual way. I might say, sir, she has no maid."

Elliott took the first half of this reply at face value. No one was better at sniffing out a mushroom than Minton. If he said she was a lady, she was a lady. But unusual and no maid? This was curious. "Tell me more, Minton," he commanded.

"Well, sir, she seems a very determined young person… er, lady. She is dressed with propriety, though not perhaps with a high degree of elegance. There is a certain amount of… er straw on her boots and her hair is not entirely… er, contained by her bonnet. But she has an air, sir, a decided air." And he ended with what was almost a tone of defiance, "I liked her. Her name, I understand, is Wilhelmina."

"Good Lord, she did make an impression, Minton. I've never heard you say you actually *liked* any young lady who has visited this house before, much less one called Wilhelmina. I have to see her." Lord Devin never did anything precipitously, so he did not leap out of bed. Nevertheless, his valet was astonished to see him so quickly upright. "Tell her I'll be down as soon as I can, Minton. Offer her a glass of wine or something. Well, don't just stand there, Thompson. You heard what the man said. Miss Chatterton is in a hurry."

It was more than half an hour before Lord Devin saw his visitor, but any of his friends would have laid odds against his being so rapid. He entered the drawing room and came towards her. If she appeared somewhat ill-kempt, he most certainly did not. His coat fit to perfection, the collar of his spotless white shirt was starched to precisely the right degree of stiffness and the folds of his neckcloth (he had discarded the ones that were troubling him) were a thing of beauty. His Hessians were refulgent and his wavy hair in the most perfect disorder.

Miss Chatterton stood and Lord Devin executed a graceful bow. He saw she had been looking at the advertisement pages of the *London Gazette* from a day or so before. He briefly wondered why it was still in the drawing room.

"Miss Chatterton," he said, looking down at her from his very superior height and deciding that Minton had been quite right. She was very attractive in a wild kind of way. She had unruly brown curls with a hint of red that had probably been put into some sort of coiffure that morning, but whatever it was, it had not lasted. They fell willy-nilly from her bonnet onto her forehead and cheeks, framing a face that owed nothing at all to artifice. She had deep brown eyes with long dark lashes, a ridiculous little nose, a mouth that was a shade too wide and, as Minton had observed, a most determined chin. She looked not unlike a rather dirty china doll, for her cheek bore a dark smudge, and Elliott noticed that it was not only her boots that bore traces of straw. Her serviceable cloak had bits and pieces sticking from it as well.

"Elliott Devin," he said. "How may I be of service to you?"

"Wilhelmina Chatterton," replied his guest, removing a well-worn glove and holding out her hand, which he gracefully bowed over. "Though I'm usually called Nina."

Then she continued tartly, "You, Lord Devin, may be of service to me by ceasing to put advertisements in the newspaper to sell your horses when you have ridden them lame and have no more use for them."

She removed her hand, which he was still holding, staring at her in a bemused fashion, and picked up the *London Gazette*. She thrust it at him, pointing at the offending column.

Sure enough, looking at where her (dirty, it must be said) finger was pointing, he read:

Selling a Good Riding Horse,
Now Superfluous to Requirements.
Buyers May Address Themselves to the
Stables in the Mews of
Number 11 Grosvenor Square.

"I found this advertisement from a couple of days ago. You will not deny, I hope, that this is your address! If the poor animal had been useful as a riding horse, no doubt you would have put it up at Tattersall's," said Miss Chatterton, with a light kindling in her eyes. "The fact you advertised it here shows you were expecting to sell it to anyone to use it in any way they liked. I yesterday rescued what I believe to be this horse from a drayman who was too stupid to see it had an ulcerated hoof and was in dreadful pain." Her brown eyes filled with tears which she angrily brushed away, continuing with increasing passion. "Your stables sold the suffering animal as simply needing to be re-shod. It was the purest chance I saw it in the street and was able to buy it from the brute who would have continued to whip it even though it could not move. It was cruelty of the worst kind. I have come to tell you that I am making a report on the matter to the Constabulary. You must know that last year Parliament passed a law making cruelty to animals punishable by a fine. The fine will no doubt be risible to a man of your wealth and consequence but I imagine an article in the newspaper mentioning you by name will not be so laughable."

Lord Devin was struck less by Miss Chatterton's threat of unpleasant publicity than by the fire in her eyes that flamed as her passion grew. She was not of an imposing stature, but as she spoke, throwing back her shoulders back and raising her chin, he found it impossible to take his gaze off her.

"My dear Miss Chatterton, you must know I do not deal with the day-to-day running of my stables," he said after a moment to collect his thoughts. "I have a large number of horses. I am completely ignorant of this advertisement, and, in fact, surprised, since I believed our superannuated or unfit animals were returned to our estate in the country and put out to pasture."

"Then let us go at once and determine whether the animal I rescued was indeed yours. I don't know why the drayman would have lied, but one can never be sure in such circumstances. People will say anything to get out of trouble."

She fixed him with a look that gave him no doubt she was talking about him as much as the drayman.

"I assure you, I have no need to lie about such an insignificant matter."

"Insignificant matter?" she cried. "To you, perhaps, living in luxury with no doubt scores of people to dance attendance on you! But to the poor horse, it was otherwise! He was in constant pain and had nothing but misery to look forward to!"

"But I..." Lord Devin drew himself up short. Why was he arguing with this termagant, pretty though she was? Besides, he thought with a rare moment of self-criticism, he was surrounded by scores of people who did dance attendance on him. Then the thought of Minton dancing made him smile.

"I see that amuses you, Lord Devin!" Miss Chatterton was outraged. "I pity poor Lady Devin, if the contemplation of the misery of God's creatures is a source of fun for you!"

"There is no Lady Devin, Madam." He was shaken out of his habitual calm and could not stop himself. "And if there were, I may tell you at once, she would have nothing to complain about."

"That, I very much doubt, if my observation of your character is anything to go by," answered his fierce critic. "But you are wasting my time. I told your man I was busy, and I am. Let us go to the stables at once, or if you are too preoccupied with your own comfort, I shall go alone."

Elliott Devin had never in his life been told he was wasting someone's time. He was conscious of a mounting annoyance, which was rare, since he spent his life avoiding annoying situations. Miss Chatterton picked up her reticule and held out her hand for the *Gazette*, which he was still holding.

"I'll take my newspaper, if you will relinquish it. You may subscribe to it yourself, you know. It's quite inexpensive. Though if you are reduced to selling broken-down horses, perhaps I misunderstand your situation."

It was very rare for his lordship to lose his temper, and he did not do so now. But this insult at last overcame his good humor. He was angry. Nonetheless, he spoke evenly.

"Certainly," he gave her the newspaper. "Follow me."

It was most unusual for his lordship to descend the back stairs and go through the serving quarters to access the stables. If he wanted to see his head groom, he usually rode around. But it was the quickest way, and he could not wait to rid himself of his companion. The consternation in the kitchens was palpable as he strode through to the back door, an unusual frown on his face and a dab of a woman, her hair tumbling from her bonnet, almost running to keep up with him. Except for the scullery maid, who had never before even seen him in person, every one of his servants wondered if he or she had erred in some way and displeased him.

"Turner!" he called when they reached the stables, and a slight man with a visage so weathered he resembled nothing so much as a kippered herring, came running.

"Explain to me if you will, the meaning of this advertisement," he said more calmly than he felt.

Elliott gestured to the newspaper in Miss Chatterton's hand and she handed it over.

The groom glanced at the paper, but it was obvious he knew what he was looking at.

"I... er, well, me lord, I..." he stammered.

"Miss Chatterton, as she never tires of saying, is in a hurry, Turner," said Elliott without raising his voice. "Spit it out."

"The thing is, my lord, he were a fine horse and though he were no longer good for riding, we thought he could be useful for... well, someone else."

"Who is this *we* who made this decision?"

"It were Dick, the lad as looked after him."

"Bring Dick to me."

The head groom hesitated for a moment but then disappeared and came back with a tall, skinny youth in his late teens into whose ear he was urgently muttering.

"So, Dick," said his lordship. "You thought this horse was saleable, did you?"

"No I never, yer honor," replied the boy stoutly, looking up at Lord Devin with a clear and intelligent gaze in his pale blue eyes. "I said as 'ow he had a problem wiv 'is 'oof and needed fixin. But 'e," nodding towards the head groom, "'e said Champion were a good 'orse in 'is day and we could make a few quid off him."

"Champion?" interrupted Elliott. "I remember him. He was a fine horse. I had no idea he was still here in the stables."

"Yes, sir, he were a fine animal," said the groom, coaxingly. That's why we kept him around."

"Even though he was, by your own assessment, unrideable?"

His lordship's tone was even, but his eyes were hard as he looked at the groom.

"Well, yes, sir. I thought it was nothing that couldn't be repaired."

"And did you take steps to... er, repair him?"

"Well, we rested him and built him up with good fodder."

"Did that resolve the problem with his hoof?"

"Er... no, sir."

"So you sold him on as needing only to be reshod?"

"Well, sir I thought there was no point keeping him on eating you out of house and home."

"And it did not occur to you to have him taken down to Uplands with the other old horses?"

"He wasn't that old, sir."

"I see. You thought to make money for me instead of costing me the price of his fodder?"

"Exactly, sir." The groom appeared relieved that his lordship understood the purity of his motivation.

"And where is this money?"

"Money, sir?"

"That you made by selling my horse."

"Well, I, er... I put it in the kitty."

"So next month when I review the stable ledger and accounts I shall find the mention of the sale for the sum of... how much was it?"

"Five pounds sir."

Lord Devin made as if to turn away, but then said gently, "And how many other horses have you sold in this way?

"Er..." the groom seemed to be deciding whether to deny the sale of any others. But evidently came to a decision.

"Not more than two or three, sir."

"And all for about the same price?"

"Yes, my lord."

"That is strange. I don't remember seeing that reflected in the stable ledger nor the accounts. I shall have to look again."

In fact, Lord Devin never looked at the stable ledger or any accounts. His secretary handled that tedious business and only applied to his lordship when cheques needed to be signed.

"Well, my lord," said the groom, a little desperately. "It may be I forgot to note the sales in the ledger."

"Ah, well, be sure you go back and do so." Elliott smiled. "Let's say three horses at five pounds apiece, plus five pounds for Champion. That will be twenty pounds. It's important to be accurate in these things. I shall expect to see that sum in the ledger and the accounts next time I look. Carry on. And thank you, Dick. It seems you were right about Champion having a real problem. The hoof was ulcerated. I shall expect you to keep a close watch on my other horses. We cannot have the name of Devin associated with poor treatment of our cattle. I'm counting on you."

He turned again to the head groom. "And in keeping with that, I'm sure I need not say that in the future all horses unfit for use will be sent to Uplands, as has always been the practice."

He did not add that once they got there they would probably end up as food for the dogs, but at least their end would not be accompanied by cruelty.

He turned and left, with the animal rights advocate close behind him.

"I'm sorry to have doubted you, Miss Chatterton," he said. "It appears you were correct about the practices in my stables. I regret it. But I fancy we shall not hear of such goings-on again."

"No," replied the lady, "I imagine having to repay twenty pounds from his own pocket will dissuade your groom from future fraudulent behavior. I must say, you handled that well. We all knew he had attempted to steal from you but you solved the problem without disgracing him."

"I'm surprised you approve. I would have expected you to have me turn him off without a character for cruelty to animals. But he's a good groom. I should be sorry to lose him."

"I am not so unreasonable as you appear to think me," replied Miss Chatterton. "Men have a right to work. They just do not have the right to treat animals in a way they would not wish to be treated themselves. It is a mark of a civilized society that we treat all of God's creatures with respect."

"I hope that applies to Peers of the Realm, Miss Chatterton," said his lordship with a smile. "Your remarks earlier led me to think you had a very low opinion of us, or perhaps it was just me in particular."

"You are mistaken, Lord Devin," replied the lady, looking straight into his eyes. "I apologize if I spoke with more than warranted heat, as I now see you were not responsible for the fate of that poor animal."

"Since you made me aware of inappropriate behavior going on in my stables, I am in your debt. Let us say no more about it." He hesitated then continued, "In the matter of the purchase of poor Champion from the drayman, I hope you will have your man of business send me a bill."

Miss Chatterton shook her head. "Let us say no more about that either."

"But you cannot be paying for animals you rescue in the streets and then keeping them eating their heads off! That is a sure way to ruin."

"I send them to my family's place in the country. My parents are pleased to nurse them back to health. They use them gently around the estate and the local children learn to ride on those that are suitable."

"Nonetheless, Miss Chatterton, it cannot be an enterprise that is without cost to you and your family. I would be happier if you would allow me to repay you."

"You can do so by intervening if you see an animal being mistreated. That would repay me more than any money."

Lord Devin would have preferred a quick financial transaction. He liked a quiet life and avoided all confrontation. The idea that he would actually intervene in someone else's affairs was anathema to him. But he nodded.

They had by now arrived at the street in front of Devin House. Lord Devin looked around.

"I see you have no carriage, Miss Chatterton. I wish you had mentioned it while we were in the stables. I would have had them pole up the horses."

"There is no need. I can easily walk to where I am going. I am attending a talk by the Reverend Arthur Broome on the subject of furthering the fight for animal rights. We have had some success with the passing of last year's Act in Parliament, but much more needs to be done. It is just around the corner. Good day, my lord."

"In that case, good day, Miss Chatterton." He smiled and bowed, and she was gone.

Chapter Four

That evening Lord Devin went to a ball at Lady Leuven's. He was almost on time. The dancing had only been in progress an hour when he entered the ballroom, immaculate in white satin knee britches, a swallow-tailed coat and a neckcloth tied with such perfection that the gentlemen were as entranced as the ladies. He watched with languid interest as Hermione Underwood elegantly danced the Boulanger with a tall, handsome army officer, no longer very young, in a Dragoon's uniform with elaborately bullioned epaulettes. The set came to an end, and after the soldier had led Hermione to a chair, Elliott approached them.

"Will you present me to this officer, Miss Underwood?"

Hermione looked from one to the other with her wide, calm gaze. "Lord Devin, this is Colonel Mitchell Gaynor, of the 11th Light Dragoons. Do I have that right, Colonel? I'm afraid I find the numbers of the Regiments quite confusing. He has recently returned from India."

"You are perfect in all respects, Miss Underwood," replied the soldier gravely, and bowed towards Elliott. "Servant, Devin."

Elliott bowed in his turn, saying "Colonel," choosing not to regard the fulsome compliment paid to a woman he had come to regard as his own. "Were you involved in the 11th's celebrated action during the Peninsular campaign back in the bad old days of Boney's romp through Europe?"

"Yes indeed," replied the Colonel solemnly. "We saw some good action in those days! Salamanca! The Frenchies ran like rabbits! Heavy casualties, of course, but no one will forget the Cherrypickers, I'll wager."

"The Cherrypickers?" said Miss Underwood.

"Yes, it's the nickname we earned at that time."

Devin had heard the story that the 11th Lights had earned the nickname less than gloriously through being caught by the French in a cherry orchard, but he said nothing.

Over the next few weeks, seasoned watchers of the courtship rituals of the *ton* were amused to see Elliott Devin and Colonel Gaynor engaged in a *pas de deux* dance around the lovely Miss Underwood. To be sure, there was no noticeable change in his lordship's behavior. Though he invariably found the soldier gravely paying court to Miss Underwood, Devin continued to arrive late, and would make his way to her side as unhurriedly as ever. He never rushed, never insisted, never gave the slightest hint he had a rival. In fact, he introduced the Colonel in his clubs, played cards with him and lost to him as happily as he won.

In truth, he never considered the solemn soldier serious competition. He was one of those lucky individuals who had always had what he wanted, and it wasn't until he arrived one evening at a ball to find the Colonel and Miss Underwood in a secluded corner of the room, their heads together deep in conversation, that it occurred to him he might, for once, have to bestir himself.

"Good evening, Lady Salisbury, (for that lady continued to act as at least a token chaperone), Miss Underwood, Colonel," he said cheerfully, breaking in upon them. "Discussing the latest *on-dits*?" Though he thought that whatever they were discussing it was certainly not that.

"Indeed not, Lord Devin," replied Hermione, perfectly calm at having been discovered in tête à tête with a handsome gentleman. "The Colonel was just explaining to me about the Punjab region of northern India. His Regiment spent many months there. It sounds perfectly wonderful, with its fertile plains and in very clear weather views of the distant snow-capped mountains."

"Er… yes," said the Colonel, much less quick at subterfuge. "And, of course, it is of political importance as the military base to support a buffer between Russia and our interests in India."

"Of course," echoed Devin. "But I see a waltz is just beginning. May I hope it is the one you have saved for me, Miss Underwood?"

Half in jest, he had made her promise to keep a waltz for him at any ball she might attend, and though she had threatened not to because of his constant tardiness, she had, in fact, done so.

"Yes," she replied. "Though I had almost given you up. I cannot imagine why you are always so late."

"My valet," he smiled, lying without a qualm. "He is both dilatory and a perfectionist. A fatal combination." He bowed to Lady Salisbury and the Colonel and led Hermione to the floor.

"Oh," said the lady. "I had rather thought it was your own dislike of hurrying."

"Perhaps you are right, Miss Underwood," he conceded with a smile. "I am the laziest of creatures. Everyone knows it."

As the dance began, she remarked, "The same cannot be said of the Colonel. He has led a most interesting life. I could listen to his stories forever."

Elliott was suddenly filled with the conviction that he had better take action, or this jewel might be snatched from him.

"May I visit you tomorrow morning?" he asked, looking at her seriously. "I have something important to ask you."

She understood. A faint blush came to her cheek. "Of course," she said, "I shall be ready after eleven."

Chapter Five

The news of Lord Elliott Devin's engagement to Miss Underwood was no real surprise to anyone, though more than one maiden heart suffered a pang. If Colonel Gaynor's heart also suffered a pang, his outward demeanor gave no sign of it. He clasped Devin solemnly by the hand and wished him well, and his bow to Hermione's fingers was a model of propriety. He understood. He was the second son of a well-to-do family. His older brother would inherit everything. Gaynor had nothing to offer Miss Underwood except his Colonel's pay. He loved her, but he knew she was worth more.

Miss Underwood herself demonstrated none of the giddy joy that might have been expected from a girl who had won the most eligible bachelor in London. Her behavior was as measured as ever and though she willingly let anyone who asked see her magnificent engagement ring, she did not flaunt it. It featured a large emerald of the first quality. The color was deeply saturated but transparent, with an elusive blue light in its depths. The jeweler with whom the Devin family had done business for generations had shown the stone to Elliott some years before.

"I'm keeping this, my lord, against the day you find a wife. Then I'll make it up into a ring of that lady's choosing," he had said. "You'll never find a better stone."

Elliott had taken his betrothed to the jewelers and she had chosen a setting. It was simple but elegant. Now it lay against her finger, the glorious depth enhancing the green in her eyes.

His lordship had, of course, sought an interview with Hermione's father who was understandably delighted with his future son-in-law. Not many people knew it, but he had made a series of unwise investments over the last few years and was far from plump in the pocket. He needed his daughter to marry well, and she knew it. She was a sensible girl. No chance of her marrying a pauper. But he had never dreamed she would capture Devin. He congratulated his sister.

"Well, my dear," he said to Lady Salisbury, "you've done us proud, and no mistake. The *ton's* most elusive bachelor for my Hermione! What a coup!"

"He was taken with her at once," replied his sister, with satisfaction. "Sought her out from the start. Then, when he saw he had competition from the colonel, he came right up to snuff. She's a clever girl!"

However, when Elliott took her to meet his mother, whom a severe case of arthritis kept at Uplands, the Devin Estate in Middlesex, her response was more guarded.

"I hope she'll make you happy, dear," she said. "I will confess, she isn't the sort of girl I thought you would someday marry."

"Why, mother, what do you mean?" he asked with some surprise. He had imagined she would be thrilled with his betrothed. Although she lived a retired life, she carried on an active correspondence with old friends in London and knew all about his liaisons. She had been urging him to settle down for years.

"I don't know, exactly. There just seems to be something a little... well, distant about her. I had a long talk with her yesterday as you know, and although she appeared open and said all that was proper, I don't feel I got to know her at all."

"Well, I think that an advantage. I'm sure, like me, you don't like the sort of people who after five minutes' acquaintance reveal their innermost thoughts."

"Perhaps you're right, dear. And anyway, it's your happiness that counts, not my silly imaginings."

Nor was Hermione as enthusiastic as he had hoped when Elliott broached the subject of his mother staying in Devin House after their marriage, rather than removing to the Dower House.

"After all," he said, "it has been her home since my father died. She keeps largely to her own apartments and all the servants know just how much to help her and how much to leave her to try alone."

"But surely," replied his love calmly, "she and her companion would be far better off in their own establishment, and if she wants to take some of the servants, she can do so. We can easily replace them, I imagine."

"But most of them have been here all their lives. I don't think it fair to put them in a position of weighing their loyalty to my mother against the desire to live and work where they have always done. Miss Wolsey would, of course, stay with her. She is devoted to my mother and my mother to her. It is she who writes Mama's endless letters for her, since she cannot do it herself."

"Of course, it shall be as you wish, my dear," replied Miss Underwood. "It's just that a house with two mistresses is rarely a happy place."

And Elliott was left with the feeling that bringing his new bride home was going to be an uncomfortable business.

To think about something else, he decided to go for a ride. The countryside was interesting at that time of the year, the hedgerows beginning to stir with life and the trees with the diaphanous veil of green they wear before their leaves fully emerge. In spite of his languid ways in town, he had always enjoyed the country. He invited his betrothed, saying he was sure the stables had a suitable mount for her. But to his disappointment, Hermione declined. She did not like to ride, she said, and would prefer to walk around the gardens or read a book.

So he strode off to the stables and the sight and smell of the horses suddenly brought his interview with Miss Chatterton to mind. He hadn't thought about her since that day. Now he wondered whether she liked to ride. He smiled at the thought of the petite virago. He looked around.

"Where are the old horses?" he asked the head groom. "The ones too old for purpose?"

"We put 'em out to grass, me lord," he answered. "Use them where and when we can. 'Course, we don't keep 'em forever. We have to put 'em down in the end."

His lordship nodded. He remembered learning to ride on an old hunter that had been put out to grass. His father hadn't believed in giving his son a pony to start with. He had mounted him on a horse in a saddle that seemed to the boy a mile from the ground.

He had been terrified the first day, frightened the next, uncomfortable the third, but by the end of the week had found his seat. Any horse he had ever been on since immediately recognized a master.

At the end of a se'enight, the betrothed pair went back to London. Miss Underwood was well satisfied with the life she saw ahead of her: mistress of a fine estate in the country and of a large London home. Lord Devin was a little less sure of the choice he had made, but he knew it was time to settle down, and Hermione still intrigued him. He had yet to see her excited by anything. But it was her very calm that made him determined to find something that would stir the passion he was sure she was hiding inside.

Chapter Six

A week or so after their return to London, Elliott was astonished to see his fiancée seated next to a person he recognized very well, but had never seen in a London salon before. A much neater Miss Chatterton was on the sofa next to Hermione, chatting gaily and waving her hands about. Her tumbling curls were contained on top of her head with a brown velvet band exactly the color of her eyes. A few had been released over her ears and curled sweetly by her cheeks. She wore a white muslin gown tied with a blue sash under the bosom and there were neat kid slippers on her feet. She looked very pretty and there was not a piece of straw in sight.

"Elliott!" said Miss Underwood, as he approached, "Allow me to present my good friend from school. Nina, this is Lord Elliott Devin, my fiancé. Elliott, this is Miss Wilhelmina Chatterton. My aunt offered to bring her out, as her family is not... up to the task."

"But," he replied, with a bow. "Miss Chatterton and I have already met."

That lady had started to her feet and now said impetuously to her friend, "Yes, I went to see Lord Devin about a horse. I was very rude to him, I'm afraid."

"A horse?"

"Yes, a poor mistreated beast for which I mistakenly blamed his lordship."

"I assure you, Miss Chatterton, that is all over and forgotten." Lord Devin gave her his charming smile and

Nina blushed. Seeing him again in less antagonistic circumstances, she realized how very attractive he was. For a brief moment she felt a most uncharacteristic pang of jealousy of her friend.

"Oh, Nina, you and your animals! I've never known such a one for trying to save them!" said Hermione, laughingly, unaware of the feelings in her friend's breast. "You know, Elliott, at school she would bring in birds with broken wings, kittens left to die by their mother; one time, even a dog that boys had mistreated. But Miss Edgebaston drew the line at her bringing the dog into our bedchamber. Nasty, flea-infested thing that it was!"

Nina had by now recovered her sangfroid. "The poor thing had been dreadfully injured! Boys had put it in a sack and thrown stones at it till it could no longer move. They left it for dead. It was just lucky I heard a faint whimper and realized what it was when we were on our walk. It just looked like a filthy pile of rags!"

"Yes, and you carried it back to school and ruined your best gown."

"Why should I care about a gown when the poor creature was suffering? And you know what a loyal companion he was when he had recovered from his wounds."

"Yes, he would follow you everywhere."

"When he wasn't in the kitchen begging for scraps! It was lucky he was such a good ratter. They were glad to keep him there when we had to leave."

Listening to this exchange, Elliott wondered that two such unlike women should have been friends. Hermione was all calm and control; Nina all passion and heart.

Later, his betrothed explained to him that Nina's family was, to say the least of it, unconventional. Her mother and father, both of good families and with personal fortunes, lived in a ramshackle home in the country where their chief concerns were their horses and the surrounding wildlife. Her maternal grandmother, disturbed at seeing the little girl growing up almost wild, persuaded them to send her to the young ladies' Academy where she and Hermione had met. Nina was now staying at her grandmother's home in London, but that lady's health was not strong enough for the exhaustion of endless routs, parties and balls necessary to bring the girl into society. Hermione had persuaded her aunt to do it. The family was not impoverished; there was money enough for all their animals and for Nina's gowns. It was just that she was more interested in the animals than in the gowns.

"She's a dear creature," said Hermione, "just in another world! She always has been. I think that's why I like her. I would like to see her safely married, but it will take someone as unconventional as she!"

His lordship thought that someone as pretty and passionate as Miss Chatterton would have little trouble finding a husband, but in response, he said, "How comes she to be called Nina? Though I must say, Wilhelmina is a burden to inflict on anyone."

"It was her great-grandmother's name, apparently. She told me when she was little she couldn't pronounce it and called herself Nina."

The two women were now nearly always together. To begin with, Hermione took the lead, as one who was not only a favorite of the *ton* but as a woman already betrothed. Nina seemed happy in Hermione's train, though she was certainly not a wallflower. Her face glowed as she expounded on the things that interested her, her curls flew and her eyes sparkled. Compared with her companion, she was no beauty, but she was charming in her enthusiasm and Lord Devin was right: it was obvious that more than one gentleman found her arresting. She soon had quite a court of her own.

Colonel Gaynor welcomed Nina in his usual courtly way. They were an ill-assorted couple, to be sure, he so tall, and she so petite, he so measured, she so full of life. The difference in their height was well enough when they performed country dances, or a Cotillion, but when they waltzed, he practically lifted her off her feet. Her laughter could be heard across the room. Once again, Elliott wondered at his fiancée's friendship with Miss Chatterton, who could not be less like her. Hermione never laughed out loud. She had a sense of humor but it manifested itself in a smile and amused look in the eyes, nothing more. However, he was still convinced that she had unplumbed depths. He was prepared to wait.

The early spring weather had settled, as it sometimes will, into a series of warm days, and in the London parks blossom was suddenly appearing all around, as if it had just been waiting in the wings for the curtain to rise. Nina sighed one day, "How I miss the country when the weather is fine! London seems so dingy!"

"But the brilliance of the salons makes up for it," said Hermione in her calm way.

"No it doesn't!" cried Nina.

"How about a picnic?" suggested the Colonel. We could all go up to Strawberry Hill. If the weather continues fine we may eat outdoors, if not, we may go inside. There we may have both manmade and natural spectacle. The park is magnificent, if a little overgrown, and the house is a little dilapidated but there are still fine things to be seen. I believe we may still view the press on which Horace Walpole printed his *Castle of Otranto.*"

"*The Castle of Otranto*?" cried Nina. "Hermione! Do you remember the copy we all devoured at school? How we trembled but we couldn't stop reading!"

"You did, perhaps, but not I," declared her friend. "I found it ridiculous!"

"Oh, yes, I remember now! You said that reading novels like that would make us all stupid. I expect you were right, but it was so exciting! I should like to see where it was printed. Do you think we could go there, really, Colonel?" she turned her bright eyes up to his face.

She looked so adorable, Elliott was a little surprised when the soldier looked inquiringly at Hermione and said, "Does it appeal to you, Miss Underwood, even though you found the book... er, ridiculous?"

"Well, yes. I've heard the villa at Strawberry Hill, although of a rather unusual taste, is worth a visit – quite

Gothic, apparently. And though I do not enjoy sitting on the ground, a picnic might be quite pleasant."

"Then let me arrange it all."

The date was set for the following Wednesday. Luckily, the day dawned bright and clear and the party was able to set out. The two ladies were in a carriage with the men riding beside them. Behind came a second carriage with a sumptuous picnic in several baskets, together with tables and chairs, and two footmen to wait on them. Hermione had said she did not like sitting on the ground, and the officers' quarters had nothing the Colonel could bring. But Lord Devin had been able to supply what was needed.

It was about an hour's ride to Strawberry Hill in Twickenham. Nina chattered excitedly all the way, and her enthusiasm brought a smile to her friend's face.

"Nina! Anyone would think you'd never been anywhere before!"

"Well, I haven't really. I didn't do a European tour like you did."

"I invited you to come with me!"

"But I couldn't leave London just then. Mama and Papa were counting on me to go to all the meetings on animal protection and to keep public interest high. The passage of the Bill was a big step forward, but there's still very far to go."

"You know, my dear, you will have to start thinking of your own future soon. You won't find a suitable husband at those meetings you go to, and I don't think the gentlemen you've met in the salons will be as keen on listening to speeches about the souls of animals as they are dancing with you."

"I don't want a husband – at least, not yet. Anyway, gentlemen don't seem to mind my prosing on about it. The Colonel, for example. Perhaps he'll make me an offer." She laughed gaily.

Hermione sat up straight. "The Colonel?" she exclaimed. "Surely not!"

"I was just funning. It's you he's interested in, not me. Anyone can see that. But since you didn't want him, it doesn't mean no one else might."

Miss Underwood's face took on a slight blush, which with her was the sign of high emotion. "I have the highest esteem for the Colonel," she said, turning her face away. "It's just that..."

"That he doesn't have as much money as Lord Devin," completed Nina.

"Oh, Nina! You know how I'm situated. My father is counting on me making a good match. I am not really free to... to marry where I chose."

"But wouldn't you choose Lord Devin?"

"Yes, yes, of course I would. I'm sure we'll be very happy," replied Hermione quickly.

But Nina was left with a sense of doubt. She was surprised at what her friend had said. Didn't she really love her fiancé? That was odd indeed. For the more she got to know Lord Devin, the more convinced Nina was he would make a very fine husband indeed.

Chapter Seven

The Colonel took his duties as host very seriously and before the trip had told them the history of the place. The grounds of the Strawberry Hill estate had been laid out fifty years before to Horace Walpole's specifications. He found the symmetrical gardens of France and Italy alien to the character of England, and preferred plantings in natural groups. Surprisingly, however, he disliked the popular idea of places designed for contemplation, like grottos and pavilions. "It is almost comic," he had once declared, " to set aside a quarter of one's garden to be melancholy in."

His grounds were therefore intended to charm the senses with pleasant vistas and walks, including a cottage and chapel in the woods one would stumble across as if by accident. This became apparent shortly after they entered the grounds. At one edge of the estate sat a curious bench in the shape of a bivalve shell. It overlooked a fine landscape. As they drove past it, Nina cried, "Oh, let's stop here! I should like to sit on that!"

Hardly waiting for the carriage to stop, she jumped to the ground and ran to the bench. Luckily, the dry weather meant that there was no puddle in the concave seat of the bench, but it was filled with blown twigs and leaves. Oblivious to these, Nina plumped herself down and swung her legs, which were too short to reach the ground.

"Wait, Miss Chatterton!" Elliott Devin strode swiftly up to her, but seeing her already ensconced said, "You should have let me clean the débris before you sat down. Your gown will be stained."

"Oh, was there débris?" Nina smiled up at him. "I didn't notice. I was entranced by the view. Isn't it splendid?" She sighed with pleasure. "How lovely to be out in the country! It's just what I needed!"

"Don't you like being in Town, Miss Chatterton?"

"Well, I've enjoyed the parties and balls, but really, nothing is better than the country. I couldn't live in London all year round."

"But who would save the mistreated horses if you were not there?"

"I know you're funning, Lord Devin, but in fact animals are the whole reason I am in London, not my coming-out. That was my grandmother's condition to having me live with her. Poor dear! She always wanted a much more conformable granddaughter!"

By this time, the Colonel was arriving sedately with Hermione on his arm. She had descended unhurriedly from the carriage and now came forward.

"Allow me," said the Colonel and used a large handkerchief to brush off the seat for Miss Underwood to sit down. Once that was done, she perched decorously on the edge of the shell.

"Isn't it lovely, Hermione? said Nina, impulsively. "I'm so glad we came. Thank you, Colonel, for suggesting it."

They all looked at the vista for a few minutes, then Nina announced, "The fresh air is making me hungry! Shall we have our picnic here? I don't mind sitting on the grass if either of you gentlemen prefer to sit in the shell!"

"It isn't healthy for anyone to sit on the grass," declared Hermione. "It is always so damp."

"But it's been dry for what seems like weeks!" protested Nina. "I don't mind anyway. I never feel the damp."

"Damp or not," said Elliott, deciding to bring this discussion to a close, "I've brought a table and chairs. We can eat like civilized people. I suggest we drive towards the house and find a suitable spot where my men can set them up."

"A table and chairs, with men to set it all up! My goodness! That's not a picnic!" said Nina. "A picnic is on the grass on a sheet or something, perhaps with pillows, if someone remembers to bring some."

"Yes, that's a very nice idea," said Elliott, "but I've never been able to eat satisfactorily sitting on the ground. Things always seem to slide off the plate. How about you, Gaynor?"

"Well, of course, I'm an old campaigner. I've eaten all over the place. If you're hungry enough, you can eat anything, anywhere, even under enemy fire!"

"Upon my word, Colonel, that makes one's objections seem so petty!" exclaimed Hermione, "I was going to say that, besides being damp, I agree with Lord Devin. When one eats on the grass one doesn't know how to hold the plate, knife and fork all at the same time, and the food invariably slides off. But compared with eating under enemy fire, that seems very little to complain about! But let us find a suitable spot for our picnic that will allow us to enjoy our luncheon in our own unexciting way, then perhaps you can tell us more about your campaigns, Colonel. I could listen to your stories all day!"

This met with everyone's agreement and the cavalcade continued towards the house. They soon found a wide beech tree that gave them both a view of the house in front and the park behind. While the footmen set up the table and chairs, the company surveyed the building in front of them. It looked like a cross between a medieval castle and a Gothic cathedral.

"Apparently," said the Colonel, taking up his role of guide again, "Walpole thought his house should develop over time, depending on the whim of the architect. I understand the interior presents to an even greater degree a variety of different styles. I suggest we visit it after luncheon."

"Bu..." Nina was about to protest that she would rather walk around the grounds, but remembered just in time her schoolmistress Miss Edgebaston's oft-repeated exhortation not to constantly put herself forward by saying what she wanted, but to politely follow the choice of the majority. So instead she said, with a smile at the Colonel, "But of course! How nice!"

Lord Devin wasn't taken in. He had noticed the slight frown before she gave that platitudinous reply. He, too, would have preferred to walk around the grounds after a winter spent indoors, but he did not like to interfere with the host's plan.

The footmen had by now covered the table in a snowy cloth. The picnickers were then served with a variety of delicious foods: cold chicken, beef rolls, leek pie, pickled asparagus and tiny new peas, finished off with strawberries and almond tarts. With it all, there was chilled white wine and lemonade. Elliott was amused to see Miss Chatterton eating heartily from everything offered to her, pronouncing it all absolutely delicious, while Miss Underwood partook very sparingly, though agreeing that the dishes were very good.

At Hermione's urging, the Colonel told them about the engagements his regiment had been involved in on the Continent and then more recently in India. They knew he had been at Salamanca, and now described the Light 11th's action at Quatre Bras and Waterloo. It was there he had been promoted to Captain. Although it had been seven years before, it was clear that to him it was yesterday. The Cherrypickers had then accompanied Wellington on his triumphant march into Paris. The Colonel described the people on the side of the road, who, a mere weeks before had been waving flags for Bonaparte, now doing the same for them, his conquerors. Nina laughed at the idea, but Hermione said seriously, "Yes, mobs are known to be very fickle."

From France, the Colonel's regiment had been sent to India and had taken barges up the Ganges to their station at Cawnpore. He had not known before arriving that the river was sacred to the Hindus and was interested to see people scattering blossoms on the surface and ritually bathing in its waters. Gold and silver fish flashed in its depths. They passed magical-looking towns with fascinating skylines and dwellings that seemed to rise vertically from the river's banks, and forests of trees he couldn't name hanging over the water.

"The vivid colors of the women's garments, the pungent scent of spices, the babble of voices in different languages," he said, "I can't tell you how it all overwhelmed me. I had never experienced anything like it. It was a completely different world and it took me some time to become accustomed to it. But in the end," he went on, "I loved it and would have stayed. But when I was promoted to my present rank I was posted back here to take up other duties. Now it sometimes seems like a dream."

"It seems like a dream to me too, Colonel," smiled Hermione. "Your stories are a glimpse into a world I can only imagine, but would so love to see!" Then her practicality reasserted itself. "But unfortunately I think we can have no more of your wonderful stories. We had best make our way to the house if we are to see it and return to London at a reasonable time."

All four were quiet with their own thoughts as the two couples made their way up the lawn to Strawberry Hill House, Miss Underwood leaning lightly on the arm of Lord Devin and Miss Chatterton reaching up to that of her tall cavalier.

Chapter Eight

The Colonel had written in advance to the housekeeper, who now showed them over the place. Even Nina was glad she had come inside. The fan ceiling in the great hall was a thing of great beauty. It was as if two rows of celestial ladies were all holding their white lace fans at arm's length above their heads of the visitors.

"How lovely!" she enthused. "Imagine sleeping in this room so that was the first thing you saw in the morning."

Since the room was totally empty, Elliott laughed. "I think I'd be more concerned with my aching back, having slept on the stone floor all night!"

"I imagine you're going to tell us that sleeping on a stone floor is a luxury compared with some of your billets, Colonel," teased Nina.

"On the contrary, Miss Chatterton," he responded seriously. "I admit I've slept in worse places, but I like a soft pillow as much as the next man!"

They were all smiling as they followed the housekeeper into the living quarters, which featured fireplaces with elaborate stonework.

"Heavens! These chimney fronts look positively ecclesiastical!" said Hermione.

"Well spotted, Miss Underwood!" said the Colonel, drawing again on his prior investigations into the place. "They are patterned on tombs in Westminster Abbey and Canterbury Cathedral. And I believe the wallpaper is meant to look like gothic stone fretwork."

Meanwhile, Nina was asking the housekeeper about the press where *The Castle of Otranto* was printed.

"Oh, Miss," said the housekeeper, "it's upstairs in one of the unused rooms, but it's been covered up for years. There's not a lot to see and I expect it's very dusty."

"Nevertheless, I should like to see it," exclaimed Nina. "The book made such an impression on me!"

"It doesn't sound very interesting," said Hermione. "I shall stay down here, if you don't mind and if one of the gentlemen would keep me company. I should like to see the stained-glass windows."

"Both the gentlemen may stay here," said Nina gaily. I'll just run up with the housekeeper. I'll only be a minute."

"Oh no, I'll come with you, Miss Chatterton," replied the Colonel. "There may be mice."

"Mice? Pooh!" laughed Nina. "I'm not afraid of mice!"

"Nevertheless, Miss Chatterton, please allow me to accompany you. I'm afraid my views of women going about alone are fearfully old fashioned."

Laughing, Miss Chatterton took his arm and they followed the housekeeper upstairs. She led them into what was, indeed, a rather dusty room, empty except for a shrouded shape at one end. The housekeeper lifted one end of the heavy cotton cloth and said, "I don't know much about printing, but you're welcome to look.

Nina pulled the cloth back further and looked at the machine. It was about two yards long and a yard wide. Wooden frames lay on top and a few rows of letters in one of them made their purpose obvious.

"Look!" said Nina, "I've seen printers at work before. They fill the frames with rows of text, ink them and put a sheet of paper on top. Then that screw there presses the plate down and prints it. How exciting! I wonder if this frame is from the *Castle of Otranto!* I wish I could read it!" But the letters were so obscured with dried ink, it was impossible to tell what they said.

Nina was poking around amongst the wooden frames when they suddenly heard a weak cry coming from underneath the machine.

"What's that?" she cried, and immediately threw herself on the floor and peered into the darkness.

"I say, Miss Chatterton! Your gown! It's frightfully dusty down there! Let me!" The Colonel knelt down beside her, just as she reached under the machine and pulled out a tiny kitten. Its mouth was open in a soundless cry, its eyes were open but bleary, its fur was matted and its ribs were clearly visible.

"Oh!" cried Nina and the housekeeper at the same time. Then the housekeeper continued, "I'm sorry, Miss. Give me the dirty thing. I told Jenkins to drown them all. He must have missed that one." She held out her hands.

"No!" Nina clutched the animal to her bosom, which was already grey with dust from the floor.

"Really, Miss Chatterton, it would be best," urged the Colonel. "The poor creature is half dead. It is the kindest thing."

"No!" repeated Nina. "He heard my voice and he used all his little strength to call to me. He deserves to be saved." She took the fine wool shawl from around her shoulders and wrapped the kitten in it.

"Do you have milk in the kitchens?" she asked the housekeeper. "I should be obliged if you would give me just a little."

The housekeeper looked doubtful but nodded and left.

Nina and the Colonel returned downstairs and found the betrothed pair contemplating a fine set of stained-glass windows.

"Elliott tells me they are inspired by the windows in King's College, Cambridge," said Hermione. "How beautiful they are!" Then, catching sight of Nina cradling the bundle in her arms, "Whatever do you have there?"

Nina unwrapped the wretched kitten and showed it to her friends.

"Ugh!" cried Hermione. "What a nasty little creature! Get rid of it! Your gown is in a shocking state, too! Oh, Nina! Will you never learn?"

"If learning means allowing a defenseless animal to be killed, no, I won't." She wrapped up the tiny kitten again.

Hermione shuddered. "Well, if you must. Just keep it away from me! I dislike cats, especially half-dead ones. We should be leaving now, anyway. But I really don't want it in the carriage with us. Can you at least put it in with the footmen?"

At that moment, the housekeeper appeared with a small bottle of milk. She gave it to Nina. "Will this do, Miss?" she asked.

"Perfectly, thank you." Then she turned to Hermione. "I have to feed the kitten. It's starving," she said, and ignoring the others, she strode quickly towards the front door and the waiting carriage.

"Oh, I don't want that creature in the carriage!" cried Hermione, running after her. "Give it to me!" She snatched the bundle from Nina's arms and brought it back to thrust at the housekeeper. "Here, drown it!"

The kitten opened its mouth wide and uttered a pitiful mew.

"No!" Nina ran back and pulled the bundle from the housekeeper's arms. "I'll ride with the footmen, if you prefer, Hermione, but the kitten is coming with me, and that's an end to it."

"Oh, Nina!" said her friend. "Will you never change? If you feel that strongly, of course you may bring the animal, just keep it away from me!"

The slightly tense atmosphere in the carriage on the way home appeared lost on Nina as she dipped her little finger into the milk and put it in the tiny cat's mouth. The kitten quickly understood and began to suck. She did this repeatedly. Then, to her amazement, the little thing began to purr.

"Oh, listen, Hermione! He's purring! He's saying thank you!"

"I should think he would thank you!" responded her friend. "Dirtying your dress and letting him suck on your finger." She shuddered. "Honestly, Nina, I don't know how our friendship has endured this long."

"Hermione! You don't mean that. I know you have a kind heart. You have always been such a good friend. I cannot believe you would have left little Horace to die."

"Horace?"

"Of course, for the author of the book!"

Hermione was forced to laugh. "You are completely impossible!"

The kitten, having sucked up all the milk, fell asleep, and the rest of the journey was completed in perfect amity. As the carriage approached her grandmother's house, Nina suddenly sat up straight, Horace still cradled in her arms.

"Oh no!" she cried. "I've just remembered! Grandmother cannot have cats in the house! They make her sneeze! I tried to bring home a stray before, but she wouldn't have it, even in the kitchens. Oh, how I wish I were at home with Mama and Papa! Horace! What am I to do with you?"

In response, the kitten opened its mouth in a soundless mew. The carriage drew to a halt and Nina leaped down, still holding him. The gentlemen had just dismounted and she ran up to them to explain the situation.

"Colonel," she begged, "won't you take him?"

"Miss Chatterton, I would if I could, but animals are forbidden in the officers' quarters. There were problems with some of the chaps having dogs and cats that ran under the horses' hooves when we were on parade and we had to get rid of them all. Caused no end of a fuss, I can tell you!"

Nina turned her appealing gaze up to Elliott.

He couldn't ignore it. "Oh, very well, Miss Chatterton," he said, accepting the inevitable. "Give him to me."

"Horace," said Nina to the kitten. "Go to your new master and be good." She kissed its bedraggled little face and handed it over, still wrapped in the shawl. Then she gave the empty bottle to his lordship. "Please have your housekeeper fill this with milk. You must feed him every two hours. Dip your little finger in the milk and let him suck. Every two hours, mind! And please do it yourself. He must not feel abandoned again. He'll think you're his mother and he will feel safe. Tomorrow we shall see if he's strong enough to lap. If not, we must continue feeding him another day. I shall come and see him in the morning."

"Every two hours?" repeated Lord Devin, bemused. "Myself? His mother?" He thanked God he hadn't accepted that dinner invitation at Lady Forbes'. He placed the bundle of cat and shawl in one of the capacious pockets of his riding duster, before bowing his goodbyes and turning to re-mount his horse. "God help us both, Horace," he said.

Chapter Nine

Arriving at home, Elliott astonished Minton by refusing to relinquish the dirty shawl and its contents he removed from one coat pocket and the empty bottle he removed from the other.

"No," he said. "Within this inelegant bundle is an animal rejoicing in the name of Horace. I am to feed him every two hours. Please have this bottle refilled with milk. He is to think I'm his mother."

He went into the drawing room and sat down with the bundle on his lap. Though somewhat shaken, from habit Minton brought in the decanter of sherry and poured the usual pre-prandial glass.

"You had best tell Cook to make me a few sandwiches to eat here," said his lordship. I think dinner at the dining table is out of the question."

If Minton had been shaken before, these words delivered a powerful shock. However, years of training left his face impassive. He bowed and left, wondering whether his lordship might be losing his mind. As far as he was aware, there had never been any madness in the Devin family, but one never knew. He did not, however, convey this worry to the kitchen when he delivered the extraordinary message.

"Sandwiches?" said the cook. "And me with the loveliest capon you ever saw just roasting nicely for his lordship."

"He has asked for sandwiches, Mrs. Watson," said Minton firmly, "and it's not for you or me to question his reason."

Back in the drawing room, the reason had suddenly pushed its head out of the dirty bundle and appeared with its characteristic wide-open mouth. But this time, it gave a small mew. The milk had obviously not been delivered a moment too soon.

"Ah! Good evening, Horace," said his lordship. "I'm assuming you would prefer a drop of this," he showed the bottle of milk, "to a glass of my excellent sherry? I cannot help but think you are making a mistake, but no doubt you know your own mind."

Dipping the little finger of his left hand into the milk and allowing the kitten to suck from it, Elliott was able to use his right hand to pour himself another glass of sherry. Thus, both man and animal were quietly happy for some minutes, until Minton reappeared with a plate of roast beef sandwiches and a bottle of Burgundy on a silver tray. When he saw the kitten sucking on his lordship's finger, he gave a start and nearly dropped it.

"Buck up, Minton! I told you," said Elliott, "I am to be this creature's mother. Miss Chatterton requires it."

Recovering his sangfroid, the butler asked "Would that be the Miss Chatterton who... er, visited several weeks ago?"

"Ah, yes, I remember, Minton. You were rather taken with her. Well, she has given me the responsibility of caring for Horace here, and I dare not let her down. You know how she is!"

"Indeed, sir. A most... er, determined young lady."

"And her protégé here is equally determined to devour the end of my finger, it appears."

The kitten had discovered that the end of his lordship's finger no longer provided the sustenance he needed and opened his mouth wide again in a protesting mew.

"Patience, Horace!" rebuked his lordship. "A gentleman never makes demands in such an obvious fashion."

He dipped his finger in the milk and put it in the imperative kitten's mouth. This process was repeated until his lordship felt his finger being released and heard the distinct sound of purring coming from the bedraggled bundle. His lordship withdrew his hand and patted the tiny head.

Suddenly, he said, "I think, Minton, Mr. Horace here may have disgraced himself. Please find something dry for me to wrap in him."

"May I take him away and... er, tidy him, my lord?"

"No. Miss Chatterton entrusted him to me. Just bring me something dry to wrap him in."

"Very good, my lord." Minton bowed himself out. Once on the other side of the door he walked towards the back stairs and the housekeeper's room, shaking his head.

Meanwhile, Lord Devin slowly ate his sandwiches, rhythmically stroking the purring bundle on his knee. Why was he doing this, he wondered? The only explanation was he didn't want Miss Chatterton to carry on thinking him an unreliable, frippery fellow. But why was her good opinion important to him? What was she to him or he to her?

Minton returned with the housekeeper who went to remove the bundle on his knee. When Elliott stopped her, she said, "But sir, I just wanted to put this piece of oiled cloth around the animal before wrapping him up. It will save... accidents, my lord."

"Very well," he replied, "but he won't like it. I'm his mother, you see." He gave her his charming smile.

He was right. Horace did not take kindly to being unwrapped by a brisk hand, and having his lower regions swathed in oilcloth, even though the housekeeper padded it with a napkin. He opened his mouth wide and gave a pitiful mew.

"Would you like to change your... er, lower garments, my lord?" said Minton delicately, "while... er, Horace is being dealt with?"

"No, I'm only slightly damp," replied Lord Devin. "And if I leave him, he may feel abandoned again. Miss Chatterton forbade it. She's right, I suppose. To lose two mothers is bad enough. To lose three is a severe misfortune."

The housekeeper returned a clean, dry bundle to the new mother, then bobbed a curtsey. Minton refilled his lordship's glass then bowed, and they both left.

Lord Devin recommenced his rhythmic stroking of the bundle, which soon produced its purring. He finished his sandwiches and sat, vacantly staring into space, until Horace once again poked his head out of the top of his blanket and demanded to be fed. The rest of the evening continued with this pattern, interrupted only when his lordship rose to fetch the newspaper or light more candles. When he deposited the Horace bundle on his wing chair the abandonment provoked an immediate protest. The kitten gave the pitiful wide-mouthed mew which proved to be his response any time his adopted mother put him down or even stopped his rhythmic stroking.

"Good lord, Horace!" exclaimed Elliott. "If this is what mothering is like, I'm glad I was born a man. Do infants really require this constant attention?"

As he sat down again and applied his finger to the now nearly empty milk bottle, he wondered whether his betrothed would be so assiduous a mother. Would she sit up with a fractious infant? She was certainly not backward in saying what she wished and did not wish to do. She did not ride with him at Devin House, even though she must have known it would please him. She had not wanted to sit on the ground for the picnic, and her desires had affected everyone, rather than the other way round. She had not cared to see the historic printing press, and had asked a gentleman to stay with her to view the stained glass, so even if that gentleman had wished to see the press, his breeding would have made him accede to her wishes.

As a rule, Lord Devin was not given to reflection. If he sat alone as he was doing this evening, it was out of laziness and a disinclination to get up and go out, rather than for contemplation.

"I don't know," he said to the still-sucking Horace, "this thinking things over is quite disturbing. Let's hope we don't have to do it again."

Horace himself was thinking about nothing, his whole attention being focused on his lordship's finger.

Lord Devin went up to bed at the unfashionably early hour of midnight, carrying his purring bundle with him. He put it down on his bed while being divested of his clothing by his valet. Minton had informed Roberts of his lordship's extraordinary behavior, but he made no remark about the stained pantaloons, simply removing them from the bedchamber at fastidious fingers' ends. Horace was not so silent. Finding himself abandoned, he set up a pitiful mewing.

"You must be feeling better," remarked his adopted mother. "Your complaints are louder. But it's no use. You must allow me to get undressed and perform my ablutions, a thing which you evidently have yet to learn."

Roberts offered to take the kitten down to one of the kitchen maids for overnight feeding, but his lordship refused, asking only for another bottle of milk. As Minton had done before him, the valet went away shaking his head.

Chapter Ten

If Elliott was concerned he might not wake at the appropriate moments to feed his charge, he need not have worried. The kitten woke at regular intervals and complained vociferously enough to disturb him. As the grey dawn appeared in the sky, an exhausted Lord Devin fell asleep, while a considerably livelier Horace greeted it by emerging from his blanket. He began to explore the world around him, which included his lordship's person, especially his little finger which retained tantalizing traces of the now empty milk bottle. Elliott awoke from a brief but deep slumber to the sensation of sharp little teeth attacking his digit.

"You little devil!" he exploded. "Is this how you treat your mother? If you're well enough to bite me, you're well enough to go mousing in the kitchen."

The kitten looked up at the sound of his voice and mewed.

"Yes, I daresay the mice are bigger than you, but I have the feeling you'd be up to the job," he replied. "In any case," he sniffed, "to judge from the odor emanating from your blanket, you need to learn a thing or two about personal hygiene." He pulled the bell.

When Roberts arrived, slightly out of breath and a hair less perfectly turned out than normal due to the unusually early hour, he wrinkled his nose.

"Quite so," said his lordship. "Kindly take Horace and his wrappings downstairs and do something about it.

Someone down there must know how to teach him the rudiments of polite behavior. You may bring him back in a couple of hours. I need some sleep."

With a wrapped Horace struggling and mewing loudly in protest, Roberts disappeared. However, not more than an hour later he reappeared, carrying the kitten still crying piteously in a clean blanket he was trying his best to climb out of. His lordship was deeply asleep, so Roberts gently placed the struggling kitten next to him. Horace immediately quieted. As soon as the valet drew the bed curtains closed, the kitten crawled out of his blanket and climbed on his stiff little legs up next to his lordship's chest. There, he scraped at the bedcovers once or twice and settled down, purring. Mother and child slept.

Just after eleven that morning, Minton opened the heavy front door to Miss Chatterton. Recognizing her, he bowed her into the drawing room and said he would see if his lordship was available. Elliott had in fact just woken up to find Horace asleep next to him. He had rung the bell and was awaiting his morning tea. Roberts arrived with the tea and the intelligence that Miss Chatterton was waiting for him downstairs. Although he got out of bed immediately and began his morning ritual, Elliott was unable to make haste, since as soon as he moved, Horace woke up and tried to follow him, teetering on the edge of the bed, one paw stretched out, crying and attempting to catch him every time he came anywhere near. Several times he had to be rescued from falling from the high bed.

"For heaven's sake, Horace, this degree of self-sacrifice is quite unnecessary," said his lordship, striding to catch him for the third time. "I cannot understand the attachment you have to me. We only met yesterday. Try to moderate your emotions. I cannot be next to you every minute."

"He cried almost constantly from the time I took him downstairs to when I brought him back, my lord," said Roberts. "One of the maids put his... er, soiled napkin in a tray of earth to show him where he should go. She said that's how they trained them at home. He seemed to understand and did his... er, business, but pitiful it was, seeing the little creature standing in the middle crying. We gave him a saucer of milk and he lapped at it right enough, but then recommenced with his crying and walked around sniffing at everyone's boots but none of them satisfied him. In the end I brought him back up here. As soon as he was on your bed he stopped his wailing and settled down. It's you he wants, sir. No one else."

"How very inconvenient," sighed Elliott. "Let's hope he remembers Miss Chatterton was his true savior. Come along, you silly creature." He gathered up an instantly purring Horace and carried him downstairs to where Nina was waiting.

"He looks so much better already!" exclaimed Miss Chatterton. "You have done awfully well! His eyes are clear, his fur is no longer matted – why, you can already see he's going to be nearly all white with a black saddle and a black cap and mask, like a highwayman! And what a sweet little face!"

Elliott was stroking a contentedly purring Horace on his knee. But he replied, "He's going to be a damned nuisance, if you'll excuse my language. He cries if I move. I can't stay in all day to play nursemaid to a stray cat."

"I told you he would become attached to you! And it's no good pretending you aren't already attached to him. Look at the pair of you! But if you put him in a basket with a piece of your clothing I imagine he will be content to be left for a while. May I look at him?"

Miss Chatterton rose and came over to his lordship, whose manners dictated that he stand, but he was hampered by Horace, who gave his usual wide-mouthed protest.

"Please don't try to stand up, Lord Devin!" she cried, taking the mewing cat from his hands. She held up the kitten at eye level and said, "Horace! Behave! Oh, but you are a sweet thing!" She sat down again and stroked the little head. Horace immediately settled down and began his loud purring.

"I hoped he'd remember you," said Elliott. "That's a relief. He seems to dislike everyone else in the house."

"As soon as someone else feeds him regularly, he'll understand," she replied with certainty, then hesitated. "Anyway, I must be off. I... I only stopped in to see how Horace was doing. I... I have to go to a meeting."

"Every time you visit me, Miss Chatterton," remarked Elliott, "you are here about the welfare of an animal and on your way to a meeting." He was oddly disappointed this fascinating young woman had no desire to see him for himself.

"Oh," replied his visitor. The truth was, she found she would like to stay with him all day and didn't know whether to be glad or sorry to have a good reason to leave. "As I said before, there is much to be done. At the moment we're trying to decide what to do about a man who owns a large number of the hackney carriages in town and who buys the cheapest horses he can find to pull them. Needless to say, they're old and often ailing and he keeps them in the most appalling conditions. We have called the constabulary on a number of occasions, but they do nothing."

"You should be careful, Miss Chatterton. Rebuking a drayman and buying his horse from under him is one thing. A man with a significant investment who employs an army of drivers is another question. He won't take your interference lying down."

Nina's heart rose hearing Elliott's concern for her, but responded, "But we have the law on our side, and, I believe, public opinion. No one wishes to see animals abused, I'm sure of it."

Lord Devin was not so sure. He thought where money and jobs were concerned, there would certainly be other interests at play. He thought Miss Chatterton was playing with fire and did not like it. But he knew her to be very independent, so said no more, and simply rose when she did. He took Horace from her and saw her to the door of the drawing room, where Minton came forward.

An hour or so later, his lordship received a visit from a second lady, this time his fiancée. She was properly accompanied by a maid, who sat in the corner of the room while her mistress talked to her intended.

"I was sorry to see you forced to take in that dirty animal, Elliott," she said. "It was too bad of Nina to put the burden on you."

The burden was at that moment back on Lord Devin's knee. He had been taken to the kitchen for his sanitary offices and a saucer of milk, which he finished before demanding to be returned above stairs to the idol of his short life. He had been purring audibly but stiffened when he heard Miss Underwood's voice.

"Oh," responded his lordship, "it has been quite a salutary experience. I've never before been responsible for the survival of another creature. I imagine it must be how a mother with a young child must feel."

"But people like us are not required to stay up all night with our children," responded Hermione. "One has nurses for that type of thing, surely?"

So that was the answer to the question he had asked himself the night before. He was quite sure Miss Chatterton would not have given that response. He smiled, but said nothing.

Chapter Eleven

A week or so later, Colonel Gaynor made his apologies to his friends, saying he had to leave town for a while to visit an ailing relative. He had been called to the bedside of his aged uncle Edwin.

This gentleman was an irascible, friendless old man who had for years lived in isolation from his family. There was a rumor he had wanted to marry the woman who ultimately became his brother's wife and had severed all ties with both of them. However, over the years the Colonel had kept up a regular correspondence with his uncle. That is to say, he wrote letters to which his relative never responded. He also visited the old man whenever he could, though because he had been so much overseas, this was not often. The truth was, Gaynor felt for the old man. He had been disappointed in love in much the same way.

It was when he was only twenty and with the disagreeable feeling of not knowing what to do with his life. His older brother would inherit the estate while he would have to find his own way in the world. The traditional choices were the Church or the Army. He was a thoughtful rather than an active man, and the Church for a time seemed the better of the two. But then a new family moved into the neighborhood and with them their enchanting seventeen-year-old daughter. Amanda Price had black, black curls and blue, blue eyes. It was a devastating combination and for him it had been love at first sight. He rode over to her home every day, often bringing posies of whatever blue flowers he could find: bluebells that wept and wilted as soon as they were cut, violets that looked so pretty but needed a thousand to make a bouquet, forget-me-nots that looked like weeds when he gathered them. But love made his normally staid disposition romantic, and it seemed to him impossible to bring anything else. The girl accepted these tributes prettily and allowed him to take her hand. But when at last he gathered the courage to propose to her, she looked at him with her wide blue gaze and said,

"But Mr. Gaynor, my father would never permit our marriage. You have no fortune, you see. You talk of going into the Church, but that would never satisfy him."

"But you, Miss Price, would it satisfy you? We could wait until you are of age. It might be best, indeed, for by then I should be established."

She looked down at that and said, "But I could never marry to displease my father, and besides, I don't know if I could be happy as a Vicar's wife. I do so like pretty things, you see."

He had left her then, stunned that his angel could have such feet of clay. Within a month he had asked his father to buy him a commission and had joined the Dragoons. It was just when Britain was beginning to feel the threat from Bonaparte and the Army was anxious for new recruits. Surprisingly, it had been the right choice for him. He was tall and good-looking, and men were naturally inclined to follow him. He was thoughtful, not impulsive, and made good command decisions. He had never been a brilliant soldier, but he was calm, efficient and effective.

When he received a letter from his brother a few months later with the news that he had asked Miss Price to marry him, and she had accepted, he did not blame her. He realized how foolish he had been. A beautiful woman like Amanda would never accept a second son. Luckily, he had by then been called to duties on the Continent and was forced to miss the wedding. Then as the years went by, he found little reason to return home. His father died early on while he was in India and his mother a few years later. He had never been back home. An infrequent correspondence with his brother informed him of the birth of a son, and then another. The succession was assured and there was no place for him.

So he had turned to his uncle, who, like him, was by choice alone in the world. He kept in as frequent contact as he could. He was therefore now dismayed to receive a letter from the old man's housekeeper saying he was near death and calling for his nephew.

Leaving London early in the morning, he was able to arrive by early evening at his uncle's residence just outside Basildon. As he rode between the gates to the house, he was shocked at how dilapidated the place had become. He felt immediately guilty that the pleasures he'd been enjoying in London had prevented him from visiting his uncle since his return to England. The gates themselves were hanging off the hinges, the beech-lined path was overgrown and dank. The house must at one time have been a lovely place. It was in the early Georgian style of grey brick with a classical pointed pediment and pillars flanking the front door. But the beautifully ordered windows were so dirty no light could possibly penetrate the interior. Weeds were engulfing the crumbling front steps, and creepers were covering most of the once gracious front entrance.

Though it was obvious the front door had not been opened in months, or even years, Gaynor pulled the bell. It clanged hollowly somewhere in the depths of the house. There was a long pause and finally he could hear the grating of a rusty bolt being drawn back. The housekeeper opened one side of the double door.

"Lord bless you, Colonel," she said. "I should have told you to come to the back door. We never use this nowadays. But please come in. You'll see, the downstairs is all closed up except for the kitchens and a couple of small rooms in the back. I'll ask the boy to stable your horse. Not much left in the stables these days, but he'll see him all right."

"And how is my uncle, Mrs. Walsh?" asked the Colonel.

"Very poorly, sir, I'm sorry to say. He hasn't left his bed at all for some time, but he won't have the doctor in. You know what he's like, sir!"

"Indeed I do! Can I go up and see him now?"

"Well, it's a mite late but he'll be glad to see you."

"Now, now, Mrs. Walsh," laughed the Colonel. "Don't exaggerate. I don't think he's ever been glad to see anyone in his life!"

"There's truth in what you say, Colonel," agreed the housekeeper, "but I can tell you he gets a deal of pleasure from your letters. He pretends he don't, but if I move them I immediately asks where they are."

"Well, I'm glad the poor old thing had something he enjoyed. He didn't have a lot in his life, after all."

"You're right there, sir, but you know what they say: *as ye sow so shall ye reap*. He allowed a disappointment early in his life, seemingly, to poison him against everyone ever after."

"That's what I've been told. I always felt sorry for him, all alone in this place and not enough income to keep it up."

Mrs. Walsh looked at him strangely, but only replied, "If you're going up, I wonder if you'd be so kind as to take your bag up, sir, seeing as there's only me here in the evenings. I've put you in the blue room – at least, that's what we call it, though heaven knows you wouldn't think the hangings are supposed to be blue. Faded quite grey these days, I'm afraid. But I've aired the sheets and I'll put a hot brick in later, after dinner. By the way, I hope you won't mind taking dinner in the small breakfast room. The dining room is all under covers. Has been for years. And it will be very simple. Mr. Gaynor eats nearly nothing and begrudges any extra spending."

"Poor old man, probably worried he's going to outlive his money." He turned and went up the stairs.

Mrs. Walsh looked at his back for a moment, then shook her head and went towards the kitchen.

The Colonel dropped his bag in the Blue Chamber. In the dying light the hangings certainly looked as grey as Mrs. Walsh had said. Then he knocked on his uncle's bedchamber door, waited a moment and walked in. He was shocked by the old man's condition. He hadn't seen him in several years, of course, but he wasn't ready for what he saw now. On the white embroidered pillow, his uncle's head was nothing more than a skull. The wisps of hair appearing on either side of the nightcap were so light and sparse as to be almost invisible. The closed eyes were sunken deep into their sockets and the skin pulled so tight over the prominent cheekbones was almost transparent. The mouth was pulled inward and lipless.

"Uncle!" said Gaynor in a low voice. "It's I, Mitchell. How are you, sir?"

The pallid eyelids fluttered and opened, with a surprisingly sharp look of recognition. But the old man's words came out in gasps. "You!" he said in an accusing tone. "So... you've c... come, at I... last, have... you?"

"I'm sorry, sir. I came as soon as I heard, sir."

"Heard... heard I was d... dying, eh?" The words came out on a breath, "Looking for an in... inheritance."

Mitchell chuckled. "Not exactly, sir. Mrs. Walsh wrote to say you were very poorly and were asking for me."

"Seen... your name... in the... the Court Circular... couple of... of months ago. Knew... knew you were... back. D... didn't c... come to see m... me, o...of course. T... too b... busy sp... spending your b... blunt."

"Forgive me, I didn't know you were ailing. You should have sent word earlier. I would have come before now."

"Why... why sh... should you? A C... Colonel! I... important m... man! O... old feller I... like me. Why sh... should you care ab... bout me?"

"Me? An important man? That's ridiculous! Of course I care about you! Why do you think I wrote you letters all these years?"

"A... after my m...money?"

Mitchell laughed. "Of course, sir, that would be it! Your hidden treasure!"

"H...hidden treasure. Y... yes." He gave a ghostly laugh.

"What can I do for you, sir? Can I make you more comfortable?"

"C... comfortable?" the only man sighed another laugh. "H... haven't been c... comfortable for m... months. N... nothing a... anyone c... can do for me. Nor w... wants to. B... be off!"

"Very well, sir." Mitchell turned towards the door.

But the weak voice stopped him. "S... suppose y... you c... could tell m... me ab... bout y... your t... travels."

The Colonel turned back, drew up an old chair, sat next to the old man and took his thin, cold hand. "Well," he began. "Back in 1812..."

An hour later the old man's eyes had been closed for some time and his breathing was shallow but regular. He put his uncle's cold hand under the covers and went down to dinner.

This became their evening ritual. The Colonel faithfully recounted all the details he could remember from every engagement and post he'd ever been in, and his uncle fell asleep to the sound of his voice. But as the days went on it was clear the old man was dying. He stopped eating and could not be persuaded to take even a teaspoonful of water. At the end he lost consciousness altogether and though his reedy pulse continued for another twenty-four hours, he finally slipped away, his nephew by his side.

The Colonel arranged for his uncle's funeral in the local church. Mr. Gaynor had no friends and the only people at the service were the nosy and those he had insulted who came to gloat. There was no funeral breakfast, and Mitchell walked back to his uncle's house with Mrs. Walsh.

"Where will you go now, Mrs. Walsh?" he asked. "I know my uncle can't have made any arrangements for you. I shall see about a pension, but it won't be much, I'm afraid. I have only my soldier's pay."

"But I was hoping to stay in the house, Colonel," she said in surprise. "You'll be needing a housekeeper, I presume, and no one knows the place better than me."

"*I*, Mrs. Walsh?" he was astonished. "What has the house to do with me?"

"But you are Mr. Gaynor's heir, sir!" Then, seeing his disbelief, "Didn't you know? I made sure he would tell you!"

"No, he said nothing to me. You mean I am to inherit that great falling-down barracks of a place?"

"Oh, it's not that bad, sir. And from what he told me, there's money to go with it."

"Money? But my uncle didn't have a feather to fly with!"

"Oh sir, you are mistaken! Just because your uncle didn't like to part with a groat, it doesn't mean he didn't have it to spend! I was worried about the bills when he got so poorly, sir, but his solicitor told he was a very warm man, for all he didn't act like it. Your uncle called him in from Basildon and did a Will all proper. I witnessed it sir, along with Mary, the daily maid. I didn't know the details, of course, but afterwards your uncle said he'd left everything to you. Left you a pile, he said. But he did laugh. You know how he was, sir."

"You know, Mrs. Walsh," replied the Colonel. "I'm beginning to think I didn't!"

Chapter Twelve

Nina had attended the Animal Rights meeting she had mentioned to Lord Devin and had found it a complete waste of time. None of the other committee members had wanted to do anything that would make a jot of difference concerning the unscrupulous hackney carriage owner.

Albert Parsons had made a fortune by flooding an area with his own carriages and drivers, offering cheaper rates than the self-employed drivers who normally made their living there. In the end, they would sell up and, most often, agree to work for Parsons, earning less but glad to have the job. He used second-hand carriages, often acquired from wealthy families who replaced them due to failing fortunes or simply fashion. He bought old, broken-down horses, and worked them to death. The conditions were almost as bad for the drivers as for the poor animals. Nina had spoken to hackney drivers who told her they were forced to work 12-hour days or longer, without resting themselves or their horses in order to meet the daily revenue required of them. There were always more drivers willing to take on the work.

She explained all this to the other members of the committee, who were shocked, but reticent to approve her course of action. Nina wanted to write a letter to all the London newspapers, signed by the members of the committee, naming Albert Parsons as a man who put profits before people and animals, and even the law. But the other members had been horrified. He could sue the organization for defamation of character, he could drag their names through the courts. No, they would write to him privately and ask him, as a Christian and in the name of charity, to improve the working conditions for both men and animals.

"You are deluded," said Nina with scorn. "As if that would soften his heart! He's not a Christian! Certainly, he may well go to church on Sunday for his wife to show off her new hat, but his heart is cold as ice. He has no charity!"

She stormed out of the room, furious.

Over the next few days, Nina walked around the city interviewing any hackney drivers who would talk to her. One of them told her that Parsons' stables were north of Charing Cross, and agreed to drive her there at the end of the day.

He took her to a place that she would not have believed could exist in the wealthiest city in the world. In a filthy stable, open at both ends, about two dozen undernourished horses were standing in their own excrement, most still attached to their carriages, snuffling desperately at the ground for the odd piece of hay left they might have missed. Since they were all still harnessed with bits in their mouths, some of them had difficulty eating at all. The animals' heads were down, their whole attitude one of abject acceptance. The visible skin of many of the animals was covered with mange and sores, and what it was like under the harnesses, she could not imagine. The stink was overpowering, though Nina was so shocked she hardly noticed it. She could not bear to look but she could not drag her eyes away; each poor beast seemed worse than the last.

Suddenly she heard a cry. "'Ere, wot yer fink yer doin'?" She turned and saw a boy advancing on her, half bold, half wary.

"I'm just going to release these poor animals from their harnesses and bits so they can eat what little has been put out for them," she replied more calmly than she felt. "And since you seem to be in charge, don't you have more fodder for them?"

Having been taken for the person in charge, the boy became a little more bold. "I puts out what I got," he said sullenly. "Old Parsons, 'e only 'as a load a week delivered."

"You mean you don't have any more?"

"Oh, I gots more, only it 'as to last, don't it?"

"Then let us give them another feed. I'll have another load sent tomorrow." Nina opened her reticule and showed him a coin. "There's a shilling for you if you do as I say."

"I don't know 'bout undoin' them 'arnesses," said the boy. "Old Parsons might not like it."

"I doubt he'll be here early enough in the morning to see it," she replied. "But if he is, you can simply say a madwoman did it and you were too afraid to approach her. Now put out extra hay for these poor animals, but not too much. They are used to so little, they will overeat and make themselves sick."

The boy certainly took her for a madwoman, so her words seemed reasonable enough, and the lure of the shilling was irresistible. He did as he was bid.

As she went from horse to horse, undoing their harnesses and removing the bits from their mouths, Nina became more and more distressed at their condition. She had nothing with her to treat their wounds. What could she do? It was impossible for her to buy them all, or lead them away. She felt helpless, but more than that, angry. For the first time she saw the difficulties of being a woman, alone in a man's world. Suddenly, she had an overwhelming desire for Elliott Devin. She was sure he would help her save these horses somehow. But how could she beg her best friend's fiancé for help, especially when she knew Hermione did not at all support her cause? She had to fight back tears of anger and frustration as she worked.

She walked nearly all the way home in the same frame of mind, hardly aware of what she was doing. The filth from the stables had stuck to her boots and skirt. Her gloves were stained and ruined. With her bonnet awry, her untamed hair springing from her head, her wild stride and dirt-smeared clothing, she did indeed look like a madwoman. Her appearance was certainly enough to discourage any unwanted advances.

By the time she got to Mayfair she had calmed down enough to hail a hackney to take her the rest of the way home. The driver was, inevitably, one of Parsons' men. As she descended in front of her grandmother's townhouse and paid her fare, she asked the driver if he knew where his employer lived. He was not inclined to divulge the information, but the sight of the additional coins glinting in her hand overcame his reticence.

"I don't rightly know the number, Miss, but I 'eard as he lives on George's Street in a fine big 'ouse."

"Yes, I'm sure he can afford a fine big house with all the money he makes!"

"You're right there, Miss!" said the driver, and clicked up his tired horse.

Nina wanted to go straight to George Street but hesitated. She decided she would do best to visit the infamous Parsons on the next day; she was too tired and dirty now. She went inside and ran upstairs before her grandmother could see her. She knew she would be horrified by her appearance.

She had been invited to a rout party that evening. Her friends would be there, but seeing Lord Devin would be as painful as it was a pleasure, and after her experience of that afternoon, she decided she couldn't bear it. She dined quietly with her grandmother and announced her intention of staying in for the rest of the evening.

"You don't go to Lady Shaw's? I thought you were to meet Hermione there."

"No, I have sent her a note to say I have the headache."

"You cannot give up an evening engagement for a silly headache! How do you expect to meet a husband?"

"I don't want to meet a husband, Grandmother!" cried Nina. "I... I shall never marry. Besides, I have more important things on my mind!"

"Don't be ridiculous! Of course you'll marry, and what can be more important than finding a husband? Believe me, my dear, you will be sorry if you end up an old maid!"

"Oh, grandmother, you don't understand!" Nina burst into tears and fled upstairs. She threw herself on her bed and sobbed. She sobbed for the poor starved horses she had seen that afternoon, she sobbed because she couldn't save them, she sobbed because she knew her grandmother was right, but mostly, she sobbed because she realized the only man she would ever want to marry could never be hers.

Chapter Thirteen

Early the following morning, the stately butler who had served Nina's grandmother for years was astonished to be given a note with an address in a very unfashionable area of London written on it.

"Please send this to the stables and ask them to have whoever provides the hay for our horses to deliver a load to this address," said Miss Chatterton. "I shall settle it with my grandmother later."

The butler bowed and betrayed his feelings by not so much as the flicker of an eyelash. He knew his mistress's granddaughter for an unconventional young lady, to say the least.

A little later, a hollow-eyed Nina was ready in her smartest walking dress, her hair for once strictly confined beneath a becoming bonnet. She thought that as a member of the working classes made good, Mr. Parsons would no doubt enjoy a hearty breakfast, reminding himself daily of the old days when he had to be up and out in the grey dawn. But he would still want to control his business and would probably leave the house while a good portion of the morning was still before him. She therefore decided to visit him shortly after ten o'clock, when she judged he would have finished his breakfast and perhaps be reading the papers or looking over his accounts and enjoying his first cigar of the day.

Her grandmother would not be up for several hours yet, so Nina ordered the carriage. She wanted to arrive in style and, with luck, impress Mr. Parsons enough to make him listen to her. The driver wrinkled his brow when he was told to go to St. George's Street. He had never been asked to drive there before, though it was not far from the addresses most visited by members of the household. However, he conveyed her there easily enough, and then asked his passenger the number.

"I don't know, exactly, Timothy. Look! There's a maidservant sweeping the steps over there. Can you ask her if she knows where Mr. Parsons lives?"

The driver did as he was asked, but without any luck. The girl giggled and said she didn't know nobody, being just arrived in the city. They clip-clopped further down the street. Nina saw now it was rather narrower than those she was familiar with and the facades were perhaps a little less well-appointed, but it was nonetheless obviously a gentleman's address. Then they spoke to an older woman with a shopping basket. She was much more informative and directed them to number 30.

"I know their housekeeper," she said. "You should hear the stories she tells! All lovely in the front of the house but scraping and cheese-paring in the kitchens. Master won't spend a groat what don't go in his own mouth or on his own back. He can't keep a housekeeper longer than you can say knife. My friend is looking for another position already, and she's only been there a couple of months."

Nina stemmed the tide of gossip by hastily thanking the woman for her help, and telling Timothy to drive to number 30. Once there, she told him to wait until she had gained entrance, then walk the horses. She did not expect to be more than fifteen minutes. She pulled the bell and in a moment was giving her name and being let into the house by a man whose long-tailed black coat and narrow white collar proclaimed him the butler, and whose unsteady gait, she was amused to observe, showed him to be already under the influence of more than a morning coffee.

"H-I'll see if the Ma-aster is avai-lable," he declared, with a hiccup. He crossed to the other side of the hall and opened a door, holding on to first a hall table, then a chair, as he progressed.

Nina was left looking in amazement around the hall. Originally it must have been a classically subdued affair, with high white walls topped with an innocent frieze. This had now all been picked out in gold, while huge mirrors in ornate gold frames hung on every wall. The wooden balusters on the ends of the staircase had been replaced by gold caryatids. The floor was covered in black and white stone in an eye-dazzling pattern. Nina had, of course, never been in a high class *maison de rendez-vous* in Paris, but if she had, she might have recognized the style.

A few minutes later, the butler reappeared and invited her to follow him into the Master's study. She followed his slightly swaying form in and beheld her nemesis. Mr. Parsons was a small, ferret-faced man in his forties, a hank of greasy hair smoothed across the front of his shining pate doing its best to balance the bushy growths on the sides of his face. He was sitting like a shrunken monarch on a throne behind an enormous desk in the French Empire style. It had a glowing mahogany surface and was decorated all around with gold ormolu in classic designs of centurions and eagles.

She waited a moment but he did not stand, merely looking her up and down critically. Mr. Parsons' taste ran to women with more opulent charms. Besides, she had no maid. She couldn't be the lady she appeared to be. Not receiving an invitation to sit, Nina simply sat herself at the smaller throne in front of him.

"And what can I do for you, Miss Chatterton?" he asked, enunciating with care.

"I'm hoping I can appeal to your Christian charity, Mr. Parsons," began Nina.

"Collecting for widows and orphans, are you, Miss?" he asked. "If so, you've come to the wrong place. I give at church on Sundays, and that's enough for me. No one ever gave me nothing in me life. Everything I got, I got through me own hard work."

"No, though I think that is an excellent charity, and I'm sure you've worked hard. But what concerns me and my friends is the sad conditions in which you keep the horses you use for your business."

"Me 'orses?" in his astonishment Mr. Parsons betrayed his cockney roots. "Yer talking to me about me 'orses?"

"Yes, I visited your stables yesterday and saw the appalling conditions there. I implore you to have their harnesses removed at the end of the day, to feed them better and look after the sores on their skin." She looked at him appealingly, her hands clasped. "Dear sir, your horses would work longer for you, and willingly, if you were a kind master. You gain nothing by treating them in this way!"

Mr. Parsons puffed up his chest and looked for all the world like an angry bantam cock. So this was the madwoman who the lad had told him about when he went to collect the night's take earlier that morning.

"Well first off, I don't know by what right yer visited me private premises. I could 'ave the law on yer! And 'ow I treats me animals is me own affair. I does wot suits me and me business." His attempt to control his accent failed completely now. "Be off with yer, yer strumpet! Visitin' a law-abidin' gentleman in 'is own 'ouse wivvout even a maid by yer side!"

Nina's temper rose. She stood, her eyes flashing. "Law abiding you may be, though give me leave to doubt it, but gentleman you most certainly are not! No gentleman would address a lady in this way. Nor would a gentleman surround himself with this ostentatious display." She waved her arm around the room, pointing at the gaudy desk, the heavy gold frames surrounding oil paintings of dubious authenticity, the gold-fringed draperies and oil lamps held aloft by scantily clad maidens in spurious gold.

Mr. Parsons was proud of what he thought was his fine taste and had combed the sales rooms for the very accoutrements Miss Chatterton was now scorning. He would return home for a copious breakfast every morning after his visit to the stables. Then he would, as she had rightly guessed, repair to his study to read the newspaper, tally up his accounts and generally luxuriate in his surroundings. He had moved to this new address just three years before, after living the whole of his life in the East End slums.

The one problem had been that from the first, his wife had been overawed by the environment, so different from everything she had known all her life. She didn't know how to address the servants and couldn't be comfortable amongst such splendor. To his disgust and displeasure, she had chosen a small room in the back of the house as her own parlor, and furnished it with comfortable oak framed chairs upholstered in the same garish colors as the ones they had in their old house. She would sit there of an evening, with her foot up on the fender in front of a small fire, knitting.

Parsons realized she was an impediment to his rise in the world and was just wondering how he could get rid of her when, digging in the back garden for the beetroot she had planted there and of which she was inordinately fond, she obligingly caught a bad cold and died.

He had been a widower for a little under a year and had taken stock of his situation. If he were to rise to the heights he deserved, he would need acquaintances who knew how to act in society and would help him find his proper place there. Buying this house and furnishing it had been his first step. Now this slip of a girl was talking about his "ostentatious display". He wasn't exactly sure what that meant, but he was certain it wasn't complimentary.

"Get out," he roared. "An' don't come back."

"I am leaving," replied Nina, putting up her chin. "But don't imagine you have heard the last of me."

She opened the study door, and the butler, who had been leaning against it, both to hear what was going on, and because his legs were unable to support him, staggered and almost fell into the room. He managed to hold onto the door frame as Miss Chatterton walked past him with a sneer.

"And I recommend you replace your entirely unsatisfactory butler. He is the first person a visitor sees. He should represent the household. Although, on second thoughts, perhaps this drunken fool does precisely that."

Chapter Fourteen

The minute she got home, Nina sat down and wrote multiple copies of the following letter:

To: the Editor of... (newspaper)
I wish to bring to the attention of your readers a dreadful trade flourishing under our noses here in the capital. Mr. Albert Parsons controls a large percentage of the hackney carriages in the city. He has made a fortune these last years building an empire by abusing both the men and the animals in his employ. While he has bought a large house and lives in gaudy luxury, he underpays his drivers and works his horses literally to their deaths.
A word with nearly any hackney driver in the city will confirm the first, and a visit to his stables north of Charing Cross will confirm the second. But be warned: a strong stomach is required. When you see the evil this man is perpetrating, you will refuse to be complicit.
A way to bring down this infamous business is to avoid taking hackneys owned by Mr. Albert Parsons. If readers would ask the driver of every hackney they hail who employs him, and refuse to ride in his vehicles, we may be able to force him to conduct his business in a manner more suited to the Christian principles of humanity and charity.
It has often been said that it is the mark of a civilized society when we protect those who cannot protect

themselves. It is true that here in Britain we have carried it one step further: we have laws controlling the working conditions in our factories and the treatment of animals. But we are a civilized people, we do not need laws to tell us what is right and what is wrong. We recognize it when we see it. In Mr. Parsons' business you may see the embodiment of evil.
Yours sincerely,
Wilhelmina Chatterton (Miss)

For a moment Nina hesitated, remembering Lord Devin's warning that she might be pitting herself against a dangerous enemy, but with characteristic disdain for her own safety, she swiftly sealed the missives in envelopes and addressed them. She put them on the front hall for delivery and climbed the stairs to her grandmother's bedchamber (for that lady was not of matutinal habits) to explain why she would be seeing a bill for an extra load of hay in that month's expenses.

Meanwhile, Mr. Parsons had looked around him and for the first time had the glimmering of a doubt that his taste was not quite perfect. He was a man not given to self-doubt and it enraged him to think that not only might his interior design not appeal to those he intended to impress, but that he had spent good blunt on achieving it.

He strode into the foyer, where he found the inebriated butler half asleep in his chair, and furiously dismissed him. He then called for the housekeeper, who he roundly berated for employing him in the first place. In fact, it had not been she who interviewed the butler, but the housekeeper prior to the one she replaced. As the informant on the street had said, a number of housekeepers had come and gone since the would-be gentleman had taken occupancy of number 30 George Street, and this one was the latest. She was already tired of the cheese-paring ways of her master and she was now so incensed by the false accusation that she gave her notice, effective immediately.

Paying no attention to her protestations, Mr. Parsons jammed his curly beaver on his head and grabbed up his caped cloak. He surveyed himself in one of the tall gilt-edged mirrors with which the walls were lined and wondered, not for the first time, why they became him so ill. He knew they were the last word of men's fashion and by God, he'd dropped enough of the ready to acquire them, but even to his own eyes he looked as if he were playing dress-up. Lord Devin could have told him that the wool of the cloak was a shade too bulky, the capes too deep and too numerous for a man of his stature and the buttons too large. The hat was too big and lay too low on his brow. In fact, he gave the impression of a boy wearing his father's clothes.

His reflection in the mirror did nothing to improve his mood. He roared for his carriage to be brought round, for he disdained riding in the shoddy vehicles he hired out for others' use, but found there was no one to hear his command. The butler had fled, and with him the single footman. In the end, he had to walk around to the mews and wait while his horse was harnessed to his flashy curricle.

He went to his stables in Charing Cross. The lad who served as watchman, hired chiefly because he was underage and cheap, was afraid when he saw him. He had told his employer about the madwoman earlier; well, he had to, to explain why the horses were unharnessed. He'd already received a beating for that. Now he wondered whether he'd heard about the extra feed, which he hadn't mentioned, just hoping the madwoman was as good as her word and would replenish the supply. God knows what Parsons would do if he heard about that.

In the stable, the night horses were now standing, as miserable as the day ones before them. "You want me t'take the 'arnesses off them 'orses?" enquired the lad, trembling and trying to divert attention away from the hay supply.

"Not bloody likely, you fool!" cried his employer. "And if that woman comes 'ere again, call the constable. She's trespassing on private property! An' if I find yer've been letting strangers into the yard again I'll tan the hide off yer!"

Parsons' temper rose again as he thought of the potential loss of business during the time wasted by his drivers re-harnessing the horses.

He rode back towards the city keeping as usual a watchful eye out for his carriages and drivers. As a man who had himself consistently cheated his employers, he trusted no one to do a decent day's work. This was his normal routine. Late in the morning he would drive around for an hour or so before going home for lunch, which in his mind he still called his dinner. After his meal, he smoked a leisurely cigar and then went out for another hour. He always visited different parts of the city at different times on different days. His drivers never knew when he would be spying on them.

Today when he arrived home, already bad-tempered, he entered a household entirely unprepared to receive him. The butler had been fired and the single footman had stayed away from the foyer for fear of his employer's wrath. The housekeeper would normally have given the cook directions for lunch, but of course she was not there either. Receiving no instructions, the cook had assumed her master would not be lunching at home. There was no scent of food from the kitchens and the house seemed cavernous and empty.

Having called in vain, Parsons finally went down to the basement kitchens. It was his habit to go down there several times a week, unannounced, to check on the store of provisions. He required his housekeeper to present a list of all purchases, and this he checked against the stores. In this way, he had discovered petty pilfering. He had fired the kitchen staff three times since taking over the house, apparently unaware that no gentleman would count the packets of tea or weigh the flitches of bacon in the larder. A small amount of theft was normal, and everyone knew it.

Now there was clearly no lunch forthcoming, though the apologetic cook offered him bread and cheese. Parsons was furious, but decided to act like a gentleman in a gentleman's home. He adopted a pompous air.

"My good woman," he said, enunciating carefully. "What do you take me for? A gentleman don't eat bread and cheese for lunch. I shall repair to my Club. In the meantime, kindly find me a new 'ousekeeper and butler. I shall hinterview candidates at four o'clock this afternoon. People of your sort must all know each other."

In this, he betrayed his ignorance of below-stairs staff, for whom graduations of rank were as fixed as those of the aristocracy, and a good deal more inflexible. However, his cook happened to have a brother who could pass for a butler amongst those, like Mr. Parsons, who had little experience of such persons. He was tall, upstanding and if not of the top drawer of butlerhood, so to speak, able to speak well for himself. And his wife would make an ideal housekeeper. Beneath a deceptively submissive exterior, she had a forceful personality and controlled her much taller husband with a will of iron. The cook reckoned that between them, the women could pull the wool over Parsons' eyes and make themselves a comfortable little nest at number 30 George Street. Accordingly, she pulled her misshapen felt bonnet over her iron grey curls and set out for the East End.

As he sought to improve his social standing, Mr. Parsons had realized he needed to belong to a Gentlemen's Club. The closest person to a gentleman he knew was the young solicitor he had used in his acquisition of the George Street residence. When he had presented himself to the firm of Throgmorton and Throgmorton Solicitors, he had been assigned not one of the superior

Throgmorton brothers, but the young Mr. James Smith Esquire.

This gentleman had been brought up on the edges of gentility. His father was a country schoolmaster and he had attended a very minor school. His ambition far outran his means, and in Mr. Parsons he had at once recognized a man who could help him. His urgent need was for money; money to purchase a place in a more fashionable firm of solicitors, money to purchase a wardrobe suitable for a man on the rise, and money to move to a more fashionable address. He had understood his client's desire for all the appurtenances of a gentleman, as that was an ambition he shared. He thought that helping Mr. Parsons to achieve his goal could be profitable to himself.

He therefore encouraged more intimacy with his client than was perhaps quite proper, and upon finding out he wanted to join a Gentlemen's Club, offered to propose him for his own, the Pen and Paper on Old Queen Street. He knew perfectly well that Mr. Parsons was no gentleman, and for his part, Mr. Parsons had no idea that members of the Club to which he presented his candidacy catered mostly to solicitors and lawyers' clerks, and he was unlikely to rub shoulders with anyone more elevated than an impoverished Baron.

It was to this Club he bent his steps after leaving his home. He did not usually go there for lunch, indeed for any meals, as he resented paying good money for what he could have at home. But he enjoyed an evening brandy and smoke with the other members. He was not much of a hand at whist, but he enjoyed throwing dice. This was a habit he had picked up in his youth in the East End, where disputed throws and accusations of cheating were commonplace. They often led to some fierce bouts of fisticuffs, or worse. Here it was much more genteel, of course. The dice were provided by the house, and arguments were very rare. He had always been lucky with dice, and in general won rather more often than he lost, but he had the sense not to draw attention to his luck, and to listen more than he spoke. As a consequence he was considered a good fellow. Not from the top drawer, of course, but not a bad chap.

The true reason he did not talk a great deal was he was listening both for the way the others expressed themselves and for the financial tips they might drop. His had always been a cash business and he was entirely unfamiliar with stock exchange investments. He had every intention of moving in that direction, though. That was a gentleman's way of making money. He would sell up his hackney business and say goodbye to the East End forever.

Chapter Fifteen

Although Elliott was as charming as ever, Miss Underwood had noticed a slight cooling in his attentions to her. On the evening when Nina had failed to show up at the rout party, his lordship had arrived late as usual, and had sat by her side for some minutes before looking around and enquiring after Miss Chatterton.

"Oh, she sent a note to say she had the head-ache and would not be coming," replied Hermione.

"That seems most unlike her." Elliott wrinkled his brow. "I've never heard her complain of a head-ache before. I hope it isn't something more serious."

"Oh, Nina is never ill," said Hermione calmly. "I expect she was saving an animal of some kind and thought it more important."

Elliott laughed. "Most likely!" he agreed.

"Talking of which," said his betrothed, "whatever happened to that nasty animal she foisted on you? What have you done with it?"

"You mean Horace? Nothing has happened to him. Quite the reverse. He is growing larger every day and controls the place. It is more that something has happened to me. It seems he is unhappy in any company but mine. No matter what time I set foot over the front doorstep, he finds me and attaches himself to me. If someone has made the mistake of closing the door to the room where he is lying in wait, he puts up a screech to wake the dead."

"How unpleasant! I should not allow a dirty animal above stairs under any circumstances."

Elliott reflected on the welcome he received from Horace, who would somehow know he was home and would run into the hall with a little mew to wind himself agreeably round his lordship's legs, until admonished to stop spoiling the shine so carefully produced by Roberts.

He could now jump unaided onto his lordship's knee, and one of his favorite tricks was to leap from there onto his desk and play with the dominoes often lying on the smooth surface. Elliott and his friend Marius, who would bet on anything, sometimes had a friendly game and a bottle of port after an evening out. Horace would find a way up onto the desk and play with them, which usually meant either turning over the tiles that were supposed to be face down, or batting them onto the carpet.

One evening Marius had suddenly announced, "I'll lay you a guinea the next tile he turns over has a three."

When he won his bet, and then the next, the inveterate gambler had said, "By God, Elliott! I'll give you fifty pounds for that cat! He could make my fortune!"

"I would gladly take your money," laughed his friend, "but it would be robbery. You wouldn't be able to keep him. He'd howl continuously till you brought him home!"

Since Marius had heard the wail put up by Horace when he was shut out of the study, he could well believe it.

"Can't imagine why he loves you so," he said. "A lazier beast than you it would be hard to find. I don't believe you'd bestir yourself to do a thing for him."

"I don't need to bestir myself," laughed Elliott in return. "He finds me. We are lazy together."

It was true. The two were now spending many a pleasant hour in the drawing room, his lordship with a glass on the side table side and Horace on his knee, asleep or purring like some sort of machine. The cat was unrecognizable as the bedraggled animal Nina had found at Strawberry Hill. He had grown fast and was sleek and beautiful. As Nina had noticed from the first, he was chiefly white but had a patch of black on his back and what looked for all the world like a black cap over his head and ears and around his eyes. While he tolerated those whose job it was to minister to him, he was slavishly attached to his lordship.

Elliott therefore smiled at Hermione and laughed, "Oh, I don't know. I find Horace a good deal more congenial than a number of people of my acquaintance!"

He then disappeared into the card room for more than an hour and only reappeared to lead his fiancée into supper.

Now his lordship was awaiting a visit from his betrothed. She had written him a note asking him to receive her at three o'clock that afternoon. The truth was, her father had been pestering her about the date of the wedding. His creditors were becoming pressing. She calmly explained that Lord Devin and she had not yet discussed the matter, but thinking it over, she decided a subtle push might be in order.

With the maid who routinely accompanied her, Hermione therefore came to Devin House on a mission.

When Minton showed her into the drawing room, Devin stood and placed a protesting Horace, who had as usual been slumbering on his knee, on the floor. The cat arched its back and hissed at Hermione.

"Mind your manners, Horace!" said Elliott sternly. His visitor ignored the cat and came forward, extending her hand to Devin, who bowed over it and led her to a seat.

"It is a pleasure to see you, my dear," he said. "May I offer you some refreshment? It's perhaps too early for tea, but something else?"

"No, nothing, thank you," she said. "I rarely take anything between meals. I find a regular routine suits me best."

There seemed no answer to that, and Elliott gave none. There was a pause, then Hermione continued, "You may wonder why I wanted to see you."

"Not really," smiled her fiancé. "I imagine people in our situation have all sorts of things to discuss."

"Yes, exactly. I've decided, Elliott, that we should give a ball to mark our engagement, and I think it should be held here. This house is much larger than my aunt's, and besides, it would be too much trouble for her."

"A ball?" said Devin, in surprise. "I must say, it never occurred to me. There hasn't been one here since my mother went to live in the country. I shall have to ask her if she is up to hosting such a thing. It may be too much for her, too."

"Oh, my aunt will gladly host the ball, it's just that I cannot ask her to undertake the arrangements in her own home. There is no need to ask your dear Mama to make the tiring trip up from the country. I confess, I had not imagined she would."

"It must be her decision. I'll ask her."

"But my aunt..."

"It is very generous of her to make such an offer, but I shall first ask my mother."

Elliott's voice was gentle but firm, and Hermione saw for the first time that her husband-to-be was not as easily led as she had imagined.

In fact, it had been her aunt who had first suggested the ball and had recommended holding it at Devin House. She hadn't said so, but Hermione knew from comments she had made before that her aunt liked the idea of standing at the top of the magnificent staircase rising from the foyer to the first floor ballroom, greeting her guests as she had often seen Lady Devin do when they were both younger. She had always been jealous of the staircase at Devin house. The one in the Salisbury family's home was not nearly so grand.

While they were talking, Elliott had re-seated himself and Horace, giving the visitor a wide berth, had crept around to where he was sitting and now jumped on his knee. By habit, Elliott began stroking him.

"Elliott!" exclaimed Hermione. "Is it really necessary for you to stroke that dirty animal like that? I don't know why it should be on your knee at all."

"Horace isn't dirty," replied Devin, smiling. "In fact he spends a great deal of time on his toilet. Longer than I, I daresay. You could hold him yourself and see."

His fiancée gave a movement of protest. "No thank you! I wish you would put him out."

"I would, but he would set up such a caterwauling we wouldn't be able to hear ourselves speak."

"How very inconvenient. I'm surprised to see you controlled by a cat," said his intended archly.

"But don't you think it gives you a good idea of how I may be controlled, if that's what you call it, by a wife?" replied Elliott with a laugh.

Hermione gave a small smile but made no answer.

"Did you have a date in mind for the ball?" Elliott returned to the reason for the visit.

"I had thought the last Saturday in June - just a month from now. The weather should be fine and we may hang lanterns in the trees in the garden."

"How very romantic, my dear," he said. "Am I to hope we may find a secluded corner to ourselves, away from the lights?"

Hermione shot a quick glance at the impassive maid, who sat silently away to one side.

"You may be sure, Elliott," she said, "I should do nothing so improper. I was merely imagining that the view of the garden from the balcony of the ballroom would be very pretty."

"Of course," said her betrothed under his breath, and then, louder, "I shall write to my mother and ask if she would like to host the ball and if the date suits her."

"Please tell her I am very happy to make the arrangements. She need concern herself with nothing. It will be good practice for when I am entertaining regularly after we are married. I am free, I imagine, to have the bills sent to you?"

"Of course," said her betrothed again. It was obvious that the decision had already been made.

With that, Hermione stood, and Elliott, tucking Horace under his left arm, stood too. He walked her to the door, the colorless maid traipsing behind, and led her into the hall. She extended her hand, and as she did so, Horace thrust out his paw, his claws fully extended, and would have scratched her if Elliott hadn't pulled him away just in time.

"Horace!" he said loudly, and dropped him to the floor. The cat fled back into the drawing room.

"My dear! I'm so sorry!" cried Elliott, annoyed and embarrassed. "I can't imagine what the matter is with him. He's never done anything like that before."

"He obviously doesn't like me, and I have to say, the feeling is mutual," said Hermione, pulling on her gloves. "You will have to get rid of him once we are married."

Having seen the ladies to their carriage, Elliott walked slowly back indoors. He returned to the drawing room. Horace was lying in his chair.

"Down, you dratted animal!" said Lord Devin sternly and pushed him to the floor. He sat down. Horace immediately jumped onto his knee. "No!" said his master and pushed him down again. "You are in disgrace." He paused a moment. "All the same," he mused, "I'm not saying you don't have cause."

Chapter Sixteen

Mr. Parsons had enjoyed a pleasant luncheon at his club, and had been gratified when afterwards in the smoking room a fellow member had asked his opinion of the recent news of the merging of the *London Chronicle Newspaper* into *the London Packet.* Luckily, he had heard another member talking about it the evening before and was able to make a reply on a subject of which he knew nothing.

"Well, of course," he said, enunciating clearly but not always correctly, "I deplore the disappearance of any means of limiting public hinformation, but if the publishers can't meet their financial hobligations, there's no halternative."

"Quite so," said the other member, "my thoughts exactly."

He proceeded to regale Parsons with a long explanation that did little to add to the topic. Parsons confined himself to nodding and murmuring assent, so that by the time the discussion was over, the other member had formed a very favorable opinion of his intelligence. They parted with cordiality and Parsons rode home feeling he was making great strides.

He walked into a house with no butler to greet him or take his coat. Hearing his step, the cook appeared with the information that a Mr. and Mrs. Timkins were in the housekeeper's room waiting to be interviewed for the post of butler and housekeeper.

They looked the perfect couple. He was imposing and serious, she was small and apparently timid. They both stood when he entered and bowed or curtseyed with obsequious attention. The reasons they gave for not being able to produce references was that their previous employer, dear Lady Frampton, had been too frail to write. Then she had died, poor dear lady, and her heirs were more interested in examining her possessions than bothering with her employees.

Mr. Parsons, not acquainted with members of the aristocracy but prepared to believe that they would act in exactly that way, accepted this without question. In fact, there was no Lady Frampton. Mr. Timkins had been a footman in an Earl's household, but had been dismissed for spilling soup down the Dowager's front not once, but twice. The elevated rank of those he was serving unnerved him and when he was anxious he was troubled by a tremor that had nothing to do with alcohol. In fact he was a teetotaler. He reported this latter fact, but not the former, to his prospective employer, who nodded with satisfaction.

His wife was small and wiry, with something of the look of a cornered ferret. This scared look belied her true nature. She was strong-willed and determined, and had been known to box her much larger husband about the ears when he displeased her. His losing the job in the Earl's establishment had displeased her very much, and life in the household had for some months been very fraught. This new position was a godsend. Mr. Timkins was not unnerved by an East-End upstart, and his wife knew at a glance she could deal with Parsons. She would adopt an air of servility and meanwhile arrange things to her own satisfaction. She was a good housekeeper and knew how to wear down suppliers with her bargaining skills. Furthermore, she knew her new employer, in spite of his adopted airs, had never been accustomed to the best cuts of meat or finest linens. There would be plenty of opportunity for her to feather their own nest.

So when Mr. Parsons sat down to his dinner, which Mrs. Timkins and the cook had prepared between them, he was offered what seemed a princely array of dishes. These included a ragout they said was beef but was in fact mostly horsemeat, a stew of "fresh" two-day-old vegetables the housekeeper had acquired cheap off a trader's cart because they would not keep till the morrow, and a dish of cod's "cheeks". This was, in fact, made from fish heads. Add to that a pie of medlars and a jug of cream, and Mr. Parsons felt he was dining like royalty. He spent the evening doing his accounts and went to bed satisfied that his life had at last taken the right turn.

This feeling came to an abrupt halt the following morning when, after his usual hearty breakfast, he sat down in his study to read the newspapers. After the articles and discussions about prison reform and the abolition of the death penalty for certain infractions, both of which reforms he heartily disapproved of, he turned to the editorials and letters page. He liked to read these. In his club it was always useful to be able to say, "I read an opinion about x in the papers this morning..." and then wait to see which side of the issue the other members were on so that he could agree with them. But today he was horrified to see Nina's letter. He saw himself described as evil and, even more stinging, the house of which he was so proud called gaudy. He hastily grabbed up the other two papers to which he subscribed and, his mood swinging between anger and despair, saw that the same letter was printed in both of them.

He was not a man given to indecision, but this was an entirely new problem. He had often been called unpleasant names, but had always scoffed. Unlike Shakespeare's villain Iago, of whom he had never heard, he would have said who steals my name steals trash. But now, knowing the members of his club would be bound to read the letter, for the first time in his life he felt something suspiciously like shame. He stood up, sat down again, stood up, walked around his massive desk once or twice. He would show that supercilious little woman he was not to be trifled with, by God, he would! He just had to think how.

He decided to break with his morning routine again and go back to the stables to see what effect Miss Chatterton's letter might have had. People wouldn't really come to see his stables, would they? He was relieved when he got there and interrogated the boy that no, the madwoman had not been back, and nothing else unusual had happened. But just as he was getting ready to leave, he heard well-bred voices echoing from under the archway that led into the yard.

"This must be it," said one voice. "Look how filthy it is!"

"Disgusting!" agreed a second.

Parsons peeped around the stable wall and saw two women, not in their first youth, approaching with a look of horror on their faces. They were not fashionably, or even well-dressed in black bombazine, but he knew they were Quality. He ducked back. He certainly wasn't going to confront them.

"It's just as Miss Chatterton said," exclaimed the owner of the first voice. "The poor horses are obviously underfed, and look! They are still in their harnesses!"

"Oh, the poor things! And they've hardly any hay. This Mr. Parsons should be reported."

"Yes. At the next meeting of the committee, we shall discuss it. I'll send a note to Sarah and Augusta as soon as I return home. They will want to come and see this!"

"Come, Eliza, I cannot abide this place any longer. It is altogether too awful!"

The two women gathered up their voluminous skirts and picked their way out of the yard.

"You!" he said to the boy who had also been cowering behind the stables (the boys came and went so often, he could never be bothered to remember their names). "Un'arness them 'orses. An' give 'em a bit more 'ay." In his agitation he had reverted to his natural speech. "An' if any more o' them wimmin comes back, show 'em 'ow well you looks after 'em."

"But Mr. Parsons, sir," stammered the boy, "if I gives 'em more, there won't be any left for tomorrer!"

Parsons cursed. He'd have to pay for another load of hay. Damn that interfering Miss Chatterton. He ground his teeth. A lady born with a silver spoon in her mouth, no doubt. A lady. Then it came to him. He knew what he could do to settle the score. An ugly smile came to his face. He climbed in his carriage and drove into the City, to the business address of the young James Smith, Esq. He was quickly shown into the office, but before sitting down, he closed the door behind him.

What he proceeded to outline to Mr. Smith caused that young man's eyebrows to rise, and when he mentioned the sum he was offering for the service he was requiring, they rose even higher. But the solicitor was in urgent need of funds. He had allowed himself to be invited to Crockford's, a gambling hell whose founder, it was said, had risen from the lofty heights of the fishmonger's stall to become one of the richest men in London. It turned out to be frequented by men generally more wealthy than aristocratic. Smith was disappointed. He had hoped to rub shoulders with the *ton*, but instead he had been royally fleeced and was now wondering how he was going to meet his obligations at the end of the quarter. Parsons' proposal, while not something of which any gentleman would approve, appeared in the light of a godsend.

The result of this interview between the two men was that Mr. Smith suddenly discovered a passion for animal rights and began to go to the lectures that Nina Chatterton so frequently attended.

Chapter Seventeen

Lady Devin responded to her son's letter about the proposed ball at Devin House with a happy affirmative. She would be delighted to be hostess. Indeed, she said, it would probably be the last time she would be able to enjoy that distinction. She did not say so, but she had no illusions about Hermione's ambition when she became Lady Devin. She knew her son's wife would want to take sole possession of Uplands and banish her to the Dower House. So she was glad of the invitation. But, she said, the standing for ages that would be necessary for the hostess was more than her joints could endure, and she would need to receive her guests sitting down.

Elliott was so pleased his mother felt up to making the trip to London that he was surprised and not a little annoyed when his betrothed commented, "To be sure, having the hostess seated to receive her guests does not entirely give the appearance one might hope for, but no doubt people will make allowances."

"If being received by a hostess who is known to suffer cruelly from rheumatism and unable to stand offends some of our guests, I would rather they stayed away!" he snapped.

Hermione, realizing she had said the wrong thing to a devoted son, made haste to smooth things over. "I only meant, Elliott, that your dear Mama may herself find it unsettling. I'm sure the last time she hosted a ball here she was not as... as disabled as she is now. It must be a melancholy reflection for her."

"Not if I know my mother," replied Elliott. "Seated or not, she is unlikely to be melancholy. She has the most cheerful disposition of anyone I know, and would not for the world dwell on her infirmities. In her day, she was the most popular hostess in London, and it is only because she could not manage to go up and down the stairs as many times as one needs to in this great barracks of a place that she moved to Uplands. I was all for making her an apartment on the ground floor, but she refused. She said that a young man like me could not be having a mother into whose rooms friends might stray by mistake when they were bosky. Not that she minded my inebriated friends." He laughed. "She would rather have welcomed the intrusion. She just thought she might frighten the life out of them."

Hermione wisely let the matter drop, but reported to her aunt that the plan to have her act as hostess had unfortunately come to nothing.

"I'm not really surprised," said Lady Salisbury. "Marianne Devin has always loved a party."

"Elliott said she was the most popular hostess in London in her day. Is that so?"

Her aunt hesitated. "Yes, I think she probably was. She was so charming, you see. The champagne might be flat, the candles might smoke, the flowers might wilt or the violins might be out of tune, but nothing ever bothered her. She would flit from guest to guest with the greatest good humor, and in the end, no one noticed anything was wrong."

"Well, I certainly hope I shall have nothing like that amiss at any ball I arrange," said Hermione firmly. "It wouldn't do at all."

She launched herself into the arrangements as if she had been doing it all her life. The gilt-edged invitations were written in her perfect script, the flowers were ordered from the most exclusive purveyor in town, and the musicians recommended by no less a personage than Lady Cowper were engaged. There was no chance their violins would be flat. She and her aunt spent hours with the cook deciding the menu for the dinner before the Ball for close friends only. There would be spring lamb and young vegetables, and fruits from the hothouses. The wines would come from the Devin House cellars. Then there was the supper that would be held in the middle of the ball at about 11 o'clock. That must feature items that could be easily consumed while standing, for not everyone would be able to find a seat. Small meat pies, both cold and warm, with little fruit tarts, cakes and biscuits were customary and would pair well with the champagne that would be served throughout the festivities. There would, of course, be the customary white soup for those who wished it at the end before going home. Hermione also instructed Minton, the butler, to contact the Watch and warn them of the crush of vehicles likely on the night of the ball. He responded solemnly that he had already done so.

Next, Hermione and her aunt sat down with the housekeeper and outlined their expectations. That lady had been in the household since Elliott was a boy. She had prepared the house for many balls during the time of Lady Devin, whom she loved in spite of her somewhat ramshackle ways. She was well aware of what needed to be done. The chandeliers would be lowered and dusted, the wood would be polished till it shone, the rugs would be taken up and beaten, the ballroom itself, which had been in holland covers since the last ball several years before, would be cleaned from top to bottom and all the small gilt chairs for resting ladies refurbished where necessary. There was nothing she needed to be told. This did not, however, prevent Hermione from telling her.

Lastly, she met with the gardener and instructed him to visit the Vauxhall gardens to see how lanterns there were placed in the trees. He was to procure the same for Devin House. The gardener, who hailed originally from Edinburgh, was quietly delighted. He had for some time wanted to take his young lady there to enjoy the spectacle, but for a thrifty Scot the entrance fee, recently raised to four shillings and sixpence, was too steep. He now saw how he could go at his lordship's expense. All in all, he was the only one of the Devin staff who formed a very favorable opinion of his future mistress.

Lady Devin arrived from the country the week before the ball, and having been carried upstairs by her loving son, was ensconced in her old chambers. There she received all her friends and enjoyed afternoons of cozy gossip. She also sat through a number of sessions with her son's betrothed, who explained in detail the arrangements she had made.

"For you know, Mama-in-law-to-be, if I may call you that," said Hermione patting her hand, "I do not wish you to think I have usurped your position. I merely wanted to save you as much trouble as possible."

Her ladyship, whose head was swimming with talk of refurbished chairs, lanterns, spring vegetables and the size of the red carpet to be laid before the front door on the night, nodded dumbly. She had always left all that to the housekeeper.

She made the acquaintance of Horace, of course. This happened the minute she hobbled into the house and collapsed on a chair in the hall. Horace, who had emerged from the drawing room when Elliott came in with his mother, immediately jumped on her lap and sat there purring.

"Oh my!" said her ladyship with pleasure. "What a nice cat! I didn't know you had a new member of the household, Elliott!"

Her son bent forward to take her hand and feel her pulse. "Mama! Your pulse is a little rapid. You must lie down. Oh, Horace! He was foisted on me by a friend of Hermione's and he's a damned nuisance. Aren't you?" He belied his words by gently stroking the cat's ears.

"Don't fuss, Elliott. I shall be perfectly fine in a moment. Did you say Horace? That's an unusual name for a cat!"

"Yes, Miss Chatterton found him abandoned under the machine on which Horace Walpole printed *The Castle of Otranto.*"

"How romantic!"

"Hardly. The little mite was close to death. I had to feed him all night long."

His mother turned round eyes upon him. "*You*, Elliott? You fed him all night long? Why didn't you give him to one of the servants?"

"Miss Chatterton entrusted him to my care. I would not have been able to face her if he had died."

"I should like to meet this Miss Chatterton. She sounds quite — unusual"

"So you shall. She is coming to the ball. But I warn you, she is more interested in animals than humans."

Her ladyship said no more, but thought that if this Miss Chatterton was able to persuade her lazy son to do something as selfless as to stay up all night feeding a kitten, she must be something indeed.

Chapter Eighteen

When Colonel Gaynor returned to his uncle's house after the funeral, he was uncertain about what to do next. It seemed both irreverent and churlish to talk about his uncle's Will, though he was on fire to know if what the housekeeper said was exact. She was able to furnish him with the direction of his uncle's lawyer, so he wrote asking him to visit at his earliest convenience.

The man duly came. Rejoicing in the name of Bertram Butterworth, he proved to be a rotund, cheerful man who looked more like an innkeeper than a man of law. "Old Edwin!" he chuckled. "Gone at last, has he, the old devil? Not surprised there was no one at the funeral, he wasn't a man to make friends."

He welcomed a glass of sherry, took two healthy sips, then opened his battered leather case and withdrew a sheaf of papers. "Here we are," he said, then read in a jocular tone:

"Last Will and Testament of Edwin Fordyce Gaynor
This testament replaces any and all those preceding it.
To my nephew Mitchell Gaynor, Colonel in the 11th Light Dragoons, I leave my entire estate, to wit: my house outside Basildon, its contents, and my fortune, as will be detailed by that scoundrel Butterworth if he hasn't absconded with the lot.
I leave it all to Colonel Gaynor as being the only man I know worth a groat. He never said so, but I understood

that with his letters over the years he was trying to make up for the wrong his father did me years ago. I can't say I'm looking forward to seeing my treacherous brother again, though he and I will probably end up together in the place all devils go.
I leave it to Mitchell to decide whether he will keep on my household staff, thieves the lot of them. He may pension them off or turn them out without a penny, which is what they deserve."

It is signed and dated by your uncle," ended the solicitor, "witnessed by Mrs. Pamela Jones and Betsy Wainwright."

The Colonel sat back in his chair, shaking his head. "Well, I never wrote to him to make up for whatever my father may have done. If my mother chose him it was because he was the better man. I always felt sorry for my uncle, to tell the truth. He was old and friendless, though he brought his misery on himself."

He was quiet for a moment, staring into the past, thinking about his own lost love. It all seemed so far away now.

Then he looked up. "I suppose I should ask you what his fortune was. I have no great expectations, I must say. I just hope it's enough to bring this old house back into a better state of repair."

The solicitor laughed. "Oh, I think you'll be able to do that, all right," he said. "I can tell you his fortune was at the end of the last quarter valued at..." he shuffled some papers, "fifty-five thousand pounds. He was a canny one, your Uncle Edwin. Got in on the ground floor of some useful investments."

The Colonel stared at him. "Fifty-five thousand pounds! I can't believe it! He always made out to be at his last shilling!"

Mr. Butterworth laughed. "He was an old devil, right enough! Never let his right hand know what his left was doing, as they say. I was his man of business for years, but if he could have conducted his affairs without involving me, he would have done. He hated to let me know what he was up to! Anyway, I've made arrangements for you to withdraw funds as you need them from your uncle's old bank. They have contacts with Hoare's in London."

After another glass of sherry, the cheerful Butterworth departed, leaving Gaynor still amazed at his good fortune.

Over the next few weeks he employed an army of builders, gardeners, painters and cleaners to completely refurbish the old house from top to bottom. Once the creepers covering the façade had been cut back, the windows cleaned, and what had grown into a meadow in front of the house scythed and the shrubs tamed, the handsome old place reappeared. Inside, the rugs were taken up and beaten, the wide oak floors washed, the cobwebs swept down from the ceilings, the covers removed from the furniture, and the woodwork polished till it gleamed. The bedchambers were stripped, all the usable linen boiled and ironed, the mattresses (in which Gaynor had always complained the duck feathers felt as though they were still attached to the ducks) re-stuffed, and fires were built in all the grates. The curtains and bed hangings mostly fell apart when taken down and were replaced with new. Finally, inside and out the house looked and felt like a gentleman's country seat.

The Colonel surveyed it with satisfaction mixed with doubt. He had always imagined he would one day marry and have a family, and he supposed it was this that had compelled him to put his uncle's home to rights. The trouble was, after Amanda Price he had never met a woman with whom he had felt anything like the strong emotions of his youth. That is, he reflected ruefully, until he met Hermione Underwood. He had been drawn to her from the start. Of course, he had been flattered by her attention and interest in his stories, but there was more to it than that.

He had long since realized that the romantic response he had had to Amanda was a product of his youth. He had fallen in love with an idea, not a reality. He knew now that what he had experienced then was infatuation. He was not a man of strong passions but of steady attachment, and he thought he recognized in Hermione a similar character. Her calm and reserve were so like his own. But with only his army pay to live on, and his lack of fortune having been the source of a rebuff early in his life, he had not had the courage to approach her. The *on-dit* was that her father was all to pieces and she needed to marry money, so he understood when she accepted Elliott Devin's offer. But his disappointment had been deep. Devin had money, position and charm. What woman would refuse him? He chided himself for the unchristian wish that his uncle had died a few months earlier. Things would have been very different. But it was too late. He must look elsewhere. He was not going to repeat his uncle's mistake. He would not die a lonely old man.

He went to the headquarters of the 11th Light Dragoons in Colchester and tendered his resignation. His commanding officer was sorry to see him go; he had been a fine officer. But now he had the means, his desire to settle down and become a country gentleman with wife and family was understandable; they parted on the most cordial terms.

Back in London, Colonel Gaynor took up the social round he was enjoying before his abrupt departure. To the invitations he had missed he wrote graceful apologies, and to the rest grateful acceptances. Miss Underwood and Lord Devin greeted him with real pleasure and congratulated him heartily on his change of fortune.

"You uncle obviously enjoyed your stories as much as I," smiled Hermione. "I'm not surprised he named you his heir. I would have done the same! I'm so happy you are back. London has been very dull without you."

Her fiancé raised his eyebrows slightly but made no comment.

It soon became clear that Miss Chatterton was very much less in evidence than before. The Colonel went to two or three soirées in a row without seeing her.

"Yes," answered Hermione when questioned about it. "She receives invitations, of course, but for one reason or another she has been unable to come. She is very much involved with her animal cause, and then she has cried off at other times because of a head-ache or some other trifling ailment. I must say, she has been looking a little pale and drawn, but when I enquire she tells me there is nothing wrong."

"Oh dear, I hope there is truly no problem," said the Colonel.

"I don't think there can be," replied Hermione with her usual calm. "I heard she enjoyed Lady March's musical evening the other night. Elliott and I were not there. It is not his favorite form of entertainment, as I think you know."

Chapter Nineteen

In fact, Nina had been staying away from social engagements where she knew Lord Devin would be present. Having admitted her feelings to herself, she decided the only way to protect her poor battered heart was avoid contact with him.

It was true she had been more than ever involved with the Animal Rights Committee. Her campaign against Parsons appeared to have been successful. After her letter to the newspapers, a number of reports came in from people who had been to his stables, though more recent visitors said that the horses were now unharnessed and there was some evidence they were being better fed. She also heard people were doing as she had suggested and not accepting rides in his carriages. The audience at their lectures had grown, too, though it was still mostly made up of ladies, often spinsters of a certain age, and a few older gentlemen. But she had noticed one new member, a young man of pleasant appearance who stood out. He had bowed to her once as she passed, but so far they had not spoken.

For his part, the Colonel pondered a day or so after his conversation with Hermione and finally came to a conclusion. He wrote to Nina, requesting an interview the following afternoon. Having received a reply in the affirmative, he presented himself at her grandmother's door the next day.

Nina had not told her grandmother of his visit, and that lady had fortunately gone to tea at a friend's, so she did not see her receiving a gentleman alone, without any form of chaperone.

"You wonder, I'm sure, at my forwardness in asking for an interview with you," said the Colonel, after bowing and being asked to sit in the armchair opposite her.

"Yes, I confess I was a little surprised. Pleased too, of course," she replied with a smile. She was also surprised to see the Colonel out of uniform for the first time, but breeding prevented her from commenting. He was dressed as a perfect gentleman in a well-fitted coat, buff pantaloons and gleaming Hessian boots with gold tassels. He looked handsome, but somehow less imposing than in his regimentals.

The Colonel hesitated. "'Pon my word," he said a little shamefacedly, "now I'm here I hardly know where to begin." He hesitated again, then continued. "Since I returned to London, I haven't seen you at any of the routs or parties where I used to have the pleasure of your company, so I don't know if you have heard of my good fortune."

He proceeded to tell her of his uncle's bequest, his new home and his retirement from the army. Now she understood his civilian apparel.

"I'm so happy for you!" she exclaimed warmly. "Are you going to retire to the country? We shall certainly miss you!"

"I do plan to spend a good deal of time there, though I shall always come to London for part of the season at least."

"That sounds perfect."

"I'm glad you think so." He hesitated again then leaned forward and grasped her hands. "Miss Chatterton, Nina, I must be straight with you. I've come here today to ask you to become my wife. I believe we could be happy together. I know you love the country and your interest in animals could enjoy full rein. I... I am not a demanding man, and I hope I'm a reasonable one. I look to my wife to be a lady, a hostess and provide me with an heir, but I do not expect constant... constant attention. After a period of foolishness in my youth, I have never been a ladies' man, if you understand me. I like and respect you. I think we would deal well together."

Nina looked at him open-mouthed. When she had joked with Hermione that the Colonel might make her an offer, she had been teasing. She had received the distinct impression that her friend had a tendre for him herself and he would have been a desirable suitor had his fortune been greater. Her first instinct now was to refuse his offer at once. He was a friend, a kind man, but she didn't love him. But then, she thought, the man she did love was betrothed. There was no chance of marriage to him. At least she liked and admired the Colonel. She would be happy with her own establishment, and she wanted children. And if the Colonel wanted to spend most of the year in the country, she would be able to avoid seeing Elliott. But could she be a good wife to him when she knew her heart was lost elsewhere? But Gaynor had not said he loved her either. She knew that many unions were marriage of convenience and he had said he liked and respected her. Well, she liked and respected him. That was a good beginning.

She came to a decision. "Colonel Gaynor, Mitchell," she said slowly, hardly believing the sound of her own voice, "you do me a great honor, and I have pleasure in accepting."

"Then you make me the happiest of men," replied Mitchell Gaynor, coming to his feet and kissing her hands. "I shall put notices in the newspapers. And I invite you and your grandmother to accompany me on a trip to my home in the country. There will be many additions you will wish to make, I'm sure."

"Oh, I doubt it," said Nina. "But I do want to see the stables!"

So it was that a day later, Lord Devin was idly perusing the London Gazette when he saw the announcement of the forthcoming marriage of Miss Wilhelmina Chatterton and Colonel Michell Gaynor, late of the 11th Light Dragoons. He stared at it, then dropped the paper in his lap, where it fell on a purring Horace. The cat gave a mew of disgust and swatted at the pages.

"My thoughts exactly, Horace," said Elliott. "Now we are in the basket."

Chapter Twenty

While Nina and Mitchell were away at his new home in Basildon, the last remaining details of the plans for the engagement ball at Devin House were laid. Hermione supervised it all, from the cleaning of the silver to the counting of the wax candles. She really was an excellent mistress; it was just a pity that Devin House had for years been run along comfortable rather than strictly organized lines, and the staff began to resent her. Horace certainly resented her. He hissed when she entered any room he was in, and more than once snatched at the hem of her gown as she passed. Elliott tried to discipline him by shutting him in an empty chamber, but he would howl continuously until he was released and could run back to the knee of his god. Lady Devin found it most amusing. Hermione Underwood did not. Apart from Nina Chatterton, whom he had not seen in several weeks, and Elliott himself, her ladyship was the only person for whom Horace had any affection. He would sit peacefully on her lap. She liked it, saying the warmth of his body eased the arthritis in her knees.

Meanwhile, in the country, Nina admired the home her betrothed took her to, exclaimed on the shining interior, congratulated the housekeeper on the excellence of the linens and hangings and went immediately to the stables. The Colonel only had the pair that drew his new carriage, and the riding horse he had acquired when he returned from India. He had simply made sure the stables were suitable for them. Nina had much more lofty plans. She would bring as many ill-treated animals from London here as she could, and nurse them back to health. They could be sold to trustworthy local people. Yes, that would be very satisfactory.

"The house is perfect, Mitchell," she said smiling at him. "But we will need to do a great deal of work to the stables."

"Of course, my dear," he replied. "Whatever you want."

They walked companionably back to the house where they dined on the simple but excellent meal prepared under the direction of the housekeeper. When Nina and her grandmother climbed the stairs to bed they were both well satisfied. It was only after she shut her door and turned towards her maid that she realized Mitchell Gaynor had never once kissed her.

They were all back in London before the day of the Devin House ball, which dawned warm and clear. Nina and the Colonel were invited, of course, and were conscious that they would probably be the object of a good deal of attention because of their own betrothal. The Colonel was handsome in his regimentals, which retired officers were permitted to wear on formal occasions. Nina wore a very becoming amber silk gown that enhanced the brown of her eyes. Her glowing chestnut-brown hair was caught up in a matching ribbon, the curls for once contained, with natural ringlets falling by her ears. In spite of the disparity in their heights, they were a handsome couple.

Conscious that every preparation had been made, Hermione did not come to the house until just before the intimate dinner with family and close friends. She was absolutely beautiful in a white silk gown under a transparent overdress decorated with rows of silver floss that shimmered in the candlelight. Her lovely white neck rose from her décolleté and her abundant dark hair shone with brilliant diamond clasps. When she glided into the hall and surveyed the flowers and tall candles with satisfaction, she looked every inch the lady of the house. Elliott came forward holding out his hands to greet her and when they met, bent to kiss her on the cheek. She stiffened. Elliott drew away, a small smile on his lips, put her arm over his and led her into the drawing room.

The dinner was perfect and the service was impeccable, but the conversation somewhat mixed. From the end of the table where Lady Devin was seated, one could hear occasional bursts of laughter. Some impulse had induced Hermione to place Nina at that end, while the Colonel was at the other end next to her. Nina had met Lady Devin for the first time that evening and had found a good deal in common with her, especially in admiration of Horace, who leaped on her ladyship's knee whenever Elliott's was not available. Between them the two ladies now entertained all those around them, the one with her fount of stories from when Elliott was a child, and the other with her natural animation. At the other end, where Elliott sat with his betrothed on his right, it was much more muted. The beauties of the flowers in the park came under discussion, as did the recent concerts and productions at the opera. These topics elicited a smile and a comment, but not the enthusiasm so obviously emanating from the other end of the table. Bn the end, apart from an aged aunt who was nearly deaf anyway, a couple of uncles whose whole attention was fixed on the food before them, and the Colonel who had his eyes riveted on Hermione, nearly all faces were turned away from the betrothed couple and towards her ladyship and Nina.

When the ball began at ten, Elliott was positioned inside the door of the ballroom with Hermione on one side and his mother, seated, on the other. Out of nowhere, Horace appeared and leaped onto Lady Devin's lap. Hermione began to protest, but the guests were already being presented and she did not want to make a fuss. The cat sat there purring quietly and receiving as his due the admiring comments and occasional strokes of the visitors. As more than one person commented, he really was a very handsome cat.

Then dance cards were distributed and signed. The dance master found partners for those who had none, the musicians tuned their instruments and dancers began to cluster. Elliott removed Horace from his mother's lap and helped her to a seat where her companion waited. Then he took his place with Hermione at the front of the Belle Assemblée line, which would present all the dancers. With the women lined on the right and the men on the left, the host couple advanced up the floor, separated, went around to the bottom, crossed and returned up the middle, each with a new partner, now in a row of four. At the top, the four separated and repeated the movement, returning in a row of six. This continued until all the dancers were in a row, or in this case since there were so many, two rows. The purpose of this was to present all the dancers and, if one were to tell the strict truth, to size up each other. It was especially important for the debutantes in their first season to see and be seen.

After this, the dance master called the quadrilles, the Scottish reels, the country dances and the waltzes. This last dance had caused a scandal when first introduced from Europe at the time of Bonaparte. Even the famously amoral Lord Byron had found it shocking. But by now none but the strictest of black-clad matrons objected to a gentleman taking a lady in his arms in public.

The last dance before supper was a waltz, and it was Mitchell Gaynor who had had the good fortune to put his name on Hermione's card against it. The couple twirled gracefully together and when the dance ended, he walked her off the floor towards the room where the supper was laid out. In so doing, they passed Lady Devin, on whose lap Horace was once again sitting. They stopped to have a word with her, and as soon as Hermione approached her future mother-in-law, Horace stiffened and hissed. She stepped back, but not quickly enough. The cat caught the silver floss of her overdress and with a rending sound, tore a deep gash in it.

Hermione gave a shriek. "You wicked, wicked animal!" she cried and lunged at Horace. "I hate you! I hate you!" The cat leaped quickly to the floor and disappeared. Hermione turned to her partner, her face red with anger,

"My dress is quite ruined. I can't stay here with it like this! I shall go home immediately. Elliott will not want to leave a ball at his own house. Will you take me, Colonel?"

"Of course, Miss Underwood, if that is what you wish," he replied.

"But Miss Wolsey will sew it up in a trice, my dear," cried Lady Devin. "There is no need to leave your party!"

"There is every need," replied Hermione with some heat. "I do not want to dance in a mended gown and I refuse to stay in this house while that cat is still here. Perhaps you will tell his lordship that when he puts in an appearance."

Elliott had missed the whole episode. It was very hot in the ballroom and immediately after the waltz he had gone to open the balcony windows. Stepping outside, he had been caught by the sight of the lanterns in the trees below. Hermione had achieved her objective: the place looked magical. He must congratulate her. He was surprised when Horace came darting out and began to wind around his legs. He picked him up and went back into the ballroom just in time to see Hermione walking rapidly towards the door, holding her overdress over her arm, closely followed by Mitchell Gaynor. He strode behind them and caught up with them just as they got to the top of the stairs.

"Hermione!" he called, "whatever is the matter? Where are you going?"

She turned and beheld her fiancé with the cat in his arms. "There you are, Elliott!" she said, her eyes flashing. "And with your familiar, I see."

"My... what?"

"Your familiar. Yes, if you were a woman, one would think you a witch. You are never without that wicked animal. It has quite ruined my gown and I am going home. Colonel Gaynor has agreed to take me."

Elliott opened his mouth to protest.

"No, I don't wish to discuss it. And I shall not return to this house while that cat is still here. You will have to decide, Elliott, it is him or me. That is all I have to say."

And with that, she swept down the stairs.

The Colonel looked after her with a gaze that managed to combine dismay with sympathy. "She is overwrought, Devin, simply overwrought," he said. "I daresay she has fretted herself to cinders with all the arrangements she tells me were required, and to have her gown so cruelly destroyed at the moment of her triumph was just too much. She asked me to take her home, and I did not have the heart to say no. I hope you will make my excuses to Nina... Miss Chatterton. I shall return for her, of course."

Elliott could do nothing but agree. He followed the Colonel down the stairs, Horace still under his arm, and instructed Minton to call for Gaynor's carriage.

Chapter Twenty-One

Since no other guests were yet leaving the party, the Colonel's carriage was quickly at the door. Gaynor tenderly handed in his lovely charge up into it, then went around to the other side and climbed in. The trip started in silence but after a few minutes he was shocked to hear Hermione sobbing quietly. He could not prevent himself. He was immediately beside her, holding both her hands.

"Hush, my dear," he said soothingly. "Don't cry. I'm sure your gown can be mended, and you may wear it at the next ball."

"Oh, it's not my gown!" she cried.

Mitchell was right that she was overwrought, and in that state she had no power to hold her tongue.

"It's everything else! I'm engaged to a man who loves his cat more than he loves me! And I don't think I can love him! His passions are too... too much for me. I had begun to think we were not suited, and when you came back and told us of your good fortune, I realized I had made such a mistake. But it was too late. And now you have offered for Nina. Oh! It's all such a muddle!"

She buried her head in his conveniently placed shoulder and sobbed again.

The Colonel did not at first wholly understand what she was saying. Instinctively, he drew her close murmuring soothingly in her ear, before realizing the implications of what she had just said.

"Do you mean, if my inheritance had come sooner, you would have accepted me rather than Devin?" he said at last.

"Yes, a thousand times yes!" she cried, looking at him with bright tears still in her eyes. "Forgive me, but my father is so placed it was impossible for me to consider a man of... of no fortune, no matter how much I was drawn to him. But you must have known how I felt! Those long conversations we had, my delight in all your stories."

"Oh, my dear," said the Colonel, throwing caution to the winds as he had done only once in his life before, "I have loved you from the start! I admit, I did think you had perhaps a *tendre* for me, but then you became betrothed to Devin and I had to put it from my mind. Of course I knew something, if not the whole, of your situation, and I could not blame you. I love you."

"How I have longed to hear those words!" cried Hermione. "But what of your proposal to Nina?"

"Now I have a home to offer, I want to establish myself with a wife and family. I could not have you, and I like Nina very much. I esteem her. But my heart is not hers. I have told her my passions are not engaged. She has taken me under those conditions because she knows I will be a good husband and let her have free rein with her animals. You are right, my dear, it's a dreadful muddle, but one we cannot untangle. Even if you cry off from Devin, I cannot in honor cry off from Miss Chatterton."

"I know, I know," said Hermione, tears coming to her eyes again. "But thank goodness, at least I didn't press Elliott to set a wedding date. The Ball was intended to push things along, but it has done just the opposite. Oh, Mitchell, will we ever find a way out of this mess?"

They looked at each other in the gloom of the carriage, lit fitfully by the street gas lights they passed, faced with the hopelessness of their situation. Hermione fell again into his arms, sobbing, and he tenderly kissed her salty cheeks

Back at Devin House, Elliott decided to put Horace out in the garden. "You've done enough damage for one night, you disgraceful creature," he said. "You need to cool your heels. And I need to think about what to do with you."

He carried him outside and put him down. The cat immediately darted off. Elliott wandered down the path between the flowerbeds, looking up at the lanterns in the trees and thinking again how successful Hermione's idea had been. It was not until he was almost upon her that he discovered Nina sitting on one of the benches dotted around the garden. Horace had found her already, and was sitting on her lap as innocently as if the idea of ripping a lady's gown had never occurred to him.

"It's so hot in the ballroom, with all the people and the candles," said Nina. "I decided to come down here. It's lovely. Hermione said she was going to put lanterns in the trees. She's so clever!"

"Yes, she is," replied Elliott, unconsciously tickling Horace's ears. "But you must have missed the catastrophe of Horace deliberately ripping her gown. I'm afraid he is really in disgrace this time. Gaynor has taken her home. She would not stay with her dress in tatters and she says she will not return to the house while the cat is here.

Gaynor charged me with the message that he would be back to pick you up later."

"Oh dear! What a shame! Her gown was beautiful and so was she! I can't understand why Horace dislikes Hermione so. But perhaps he remembers her trying to have him drowned at Strawberry Hill. Animals do remember things and people. They are not nearly as unintelligent as many believe."

"Horace is certainly not unintelligent. He has the whole household, and particularly me, marching to the beat of his drum. But I can't keep him here. I shall have to ask my mother if she'll take him."

"He won't be happy. You are the light of his life."

Elliott sat down next to Nina, and Horace immediately jumped into his lap, purring. They sat there quietly, saying nothing. For Nina it was because the proximity of the man she loved was almost more than she could bear, and for Elliott it was because he suddenly realized he would much rather be sitting there with Nina than with his fiancée. He felt sure that if they had been betrothed and he had sought a tryst in the shadows with her, she would have been a willing participant.

They looked at each other, then, as these things happen, they both made as if to speak at once.

"I..." began Nina.

"D..." began Elliott, then, "please go on, Miss Chatterton."

Nina did not know how to go on. She wanted to say what was in her heart, to tell him she loved him, even though she knew it was hopeless. But, of course, she could not.

"I... I'd better go upstairs now," she said finally, in a low voice. "My absence will be remarked and I hear the musicians tuning up for the second half of the dancing."

Elliott was fairly sure that was not what she had been going to say, and knew that what had been on the tip of his tongue was equally unutterable. He had been going to ask her whether she thought he was making a mistake with her friend. But, of course, he could not.

He said lightly, "Don't forget you promised me a waltz. Though one of us may have to dance with Horace on his or her shoulder!"

Nina laughed and, rising from the bench, ran quickly into the house. Elliott sat there a few more minutes, mechanically stroking Horace and thinking. He was trying to remember why he had asked Hermione to marry him. Had he been in love? No, he now admitted to himself, it was because he had not wanted to come second in the race with Gaynor. He had told himself he would discover her passion once they were better acquainted. But now he knew that, beautiful as she was, her emotions did not run deep. She had told him at the outset her heart was well under control but, against all the evidence, he had chosen to believe otherwise. *Well*, he thought, tugging at Horace's ears, *see where your pride has got you, you fool.*

He went upstairs, carefully shutting the ground floor windows to the gardens, leaving Horace outside. He could see the cat's wide-mouthed complaint, but with the musicians tuning their instruments upstairs, the sound was lost. He had been set to partner Hermione in the first dance after supper, but instead, when he re-entered the ballroom, he sat down next to his mother.

"Dear Elliott," said Lady Devin fondly, "what a shame that Hermione was so upset. We could easily have repaired her gown and no one would have noticed."

"That wouldn't have done, I'm afraid," he answered more lightly than he felt. "She dislikes her plans to be upset."

"I see. Well, she certainly is a master of organization. I don't think Devin House has ever looked so beautiful and everything to do with the ball has been absolutely first rate." His mother looked sideways at him. "Her friend Miss Chatterton is a delightful girl. She had us in whoops at the dinner table with her stories about her dear parents and their animals. It's obvious she's very fond of them but recognizes they are a little… well, extreme, to say the least."

"She's more than a little extreme herself," he smiled. "I met her when she came here to take me to task for selling an ailing horse. You should have seen her, Mama! She was ready to do battle with me, the whole of my household, and no doubt the King himself, to see justice for the animal! And you know she rescued Horace in the teeth of all opposition."

"Then she will be an odd match with Colonel Gaynor. He seems a rather staid person."

Elliott nodded. "Yes," he agreed somewhat sadly, a fact his mother did not fail to notice. "She's throwing herself away."

Chapter Twenty-Two

Little was seen of either Nina or the Colonel over the next few weeks. He had returned to Basildon to oversee some further changes to the house, and she concentrated entirely on her work with the animal rights campaigners. The response to her letters to the press had been remarkably good and she was becoming quite well known. A couple of reporters had taken up her story and one had even published an article entitled, *Savior of Dumb Beasts. Miss Wilhelmina Chatterton speaks for those who cannot speak for themselves.*

The Colonel had frowned a little when he saw it. "I cannot say I like to see your name in the papers, my dear," he said gravely, "though I know you mean well. But I hope you will not mind my mentioning it is not quite what I would wish for in my wife."

Nonetheless, everyone now seemed to know about Mr. Parsons and his stables; scarcely a day went by without pairs of ladies (it always seemed to be ladies) visiting his premises and shaking their heads over the horses. The lad acting as watchman was making a good thing out of it. He had the brainwave of allowing the visitors, for the price of a farthing a handful, to give some hay to whichever of the animals they felt most in need. Since the hay was, after all, purchased by Mr. Parsons to feed the horses, and the visitors were only doing a job he himself would have to do, the lad did not feel he was cheating anybody. His newfound wealth was making him popular with his family, where he had previously been thought of as something of a disappointment. He was happy, the horses were better fed and the ladies who fed them went away feeling they had done something to help.

The only person who continued to be very unhappy was Mr. Parsons. Would-be passengers were routinely asking the drivers if they were his employees, and though he had told them all to deny any connection, revenues were down. His expenditure on hay had gone up and the men in his club had begun to recognize him as the person accused in the papers of using broken-down horses. More than one of them had taken it upon themselves to say, "Word to the wise, old fellow. What you do in your business is your affair, of course, but no one likes it when a Member's name is associated with this sort of thing. Best to stay out of the papers, if you can."

Nina's notoriety was such that she had been asked to deliver an address at the next lecture, and with some hesitation, she agreed to do so. She knew once she was married she would no longer be able to play such an active role. This might be her last chance. When Parsons saw her name at the top of the billing for the next lecture, he went once again to see his young solicitor. It was time for action.

Nina had no illusions that the pressure on Parsons would last unless ongoing measures were taken. This was the main thrust of her lecture. After summarizing what had been achieved so far by the committee for animal rights, she ended:

"I urge you, ladies and gentlemen, to form groups with your like-minded friends, and create a schedule whereby people visit and take notes on Mr. Parsons' premises and others like them: the yards of inns where dray carts are gathered, the shops of coal merchants and other delivery service, anywhere where horses or other animals are used, to ensure the fair and Christian treatment of them. If these people know they are under scrutiny, they will, perforce, improve the conditions for their animals, and thereby no doubt the conditions for their men as well.

For man and beast have always worked together. It was a donkey who carried our Savior into Jerusalem; it was a horse that carried our great King Henry on the field of Agincourt. We are taught that elephants carried Hannibal over the Alps. We have dogs to herd our sheep and cats to keep our kitchens free of mice. Where would we be without the animals that feed, protect and serve us? It is easy to respect something more powerful than ourselves. But it is when we treat those creatures, weaker than we are, with both dignity and respect that we reflect the Almighty in us, and His tenderness towards us, His creation."

Nina was not a commanding figure. She was, if anything, rather short. And she was young. But as she stood there, her pretty face alive with passion, her whole being filled with what she was saying, and her clear voice ringing out, the people in the audience could not take their eyes off her. There was loud applause when she finished, and a few cries of *Bravo!* notably from the nice-looking young gentleman who sat near the back.

There were some matters of business to be attended to after the talk and it was quite late by the time the meeting broke up., Nina judged it must be after six. As she walked toward the door, she was stopped by the pleasant young gentleman, who bowed and said, "Miss Chatterton, I am Paul Walker. We have not been introduced, I know, but I have waited to see you. Please allow me to congratulate you on the excellence of your talk. It echoed my own feelings exactly."

"Why, thank you, Mr. Walker. I have noticed you several times before. I believe you must be the only man in the audience under the age of fifty!" Nina smiled.

"Yes, I suppose it is rare for a younger man to interest himself in such things," replied the young man. "But you must not believe we all think only of horseracing and cards! I have for some time been aware of the need to draw public attention to the ill-treatment of our animal friends. It was my sister who first spoke of it some years ago. She is a great animal lover, but is unfortunately confined to her bed with a wasting disease of the legs. She followed with avid interest the progress of the Animal Rights Act through Parliament last year. She read your letter in the Gazette and was impressed with your courage in speaking out. When I said I had seen you several times at these meetings, she said if only she could meet you, she felt sure she would be filled with some of your spirit. Of course, we both know an important person like you must be much too busy for such a thing!"

"But of course I am not too busy!" cried Nina. "I should be delighted to meet her! Where do you reside?"

"Oh, just on the edge of Mayfair. Not exactly the most fashionable area, but one where I feel safe leaving my sister alone."

"In that case, if you have time, I could come and see her now. I have no other engagements this evening."

"I have plenty of time. I do not like to leave Maura in the evenings and rarely go out. My goodness! She begged me before I left to pay close attention to your discourse so that I might repeat it to her, but for you to do it in person would be more than she could ever have hoped for!"

"Well, I'm not going to deliver another speech, but it would be my pleasure to converse with her," laughed Nina.

"In that case, let us go. I would be honored to convey you there. My carriage is outside. It's my one extravagance, I'm afraid. Maura is always telling me I ought to give it up and take a hackney, but I confess it goes against the grain to do so." He hesitated. "That is, if you have no objection to an open carriage. But at least there can be no impropriety in your traveling with me in it alone without a chaperone."

Nina laughed. "That would be the last consideration on my mind, Mr. Walker. I find these notions of women needing constant protection positively antiquated. I usually travel alone, though I must say my fiancé deplores the habit. He is from town at the moment and I cried off any engagements. It's therefore a good moment to come and meet your sister."

She thought it was as well to make mention of her fiancé, lest Mr. Walker imagine her interest was in more than meeting his sister. Besides, it was true that Mitchell did not like her travelling around town on her own. He had spoken of it often, and although he was always very nice about it, she imagined that once she was married she would be required to always have a maid with her. She sighed, but firmly pushed the image of herself as the Colonel's wife out of her mind. Instead she thought about Mr. Walker's sister. Maura was her name, apparently. Imagine being confined to bed when one was young! How dreadful! Nina's soft heart was immediately touched. She was touched too by the young man's devotion to her – fancy spending all his evenings with his sister!

By now they were on the linkway and Nina could see the carriage that was apparently her companion's pride and joy. She blinked. Where Mr. Walker himself was correctly but soberly dressed in a dark coat with buff pantaloons and boots (though without the glassy gleam Lord Devin's man seemed able to achieve), the carriage was, well, one would have to say, gaudy. It was a perch phaeton with large yellow back wheels and smaller ones in front. The leather seat was scarlet with yellow trim. It was impossible to miss. For a moment, she wished she had not agreed to go with Mr. Walker, but then chided herself for being so stuffy. The linkboy was handing the reins to Mr. Walker and receiving a coin for his trouble. Nina couldn't help noticing it was a sixpence. That was generous! Her companion helped her up onto the high seat and went around to take his place on the other side.

Nina was not in the habit of driving in perch phaetons or indeed any other form of sporting open carriage with a gentleman handing the reins. Her parents had a gig which she or they took when needed, otherwise they had a lumbering old coach which the coachman drove with slow, solemn dignity. Her grandmother's coachman was cut from the same cloth. He knew what was due to a woman of advanced years and drove the same way even when Nina was the only passenger. But she was forced to the conclusion that, attached though he may be to his carriage, Mr. Walker was far from expert in driving it. He appeared ill at ease and hesitant, jabbing at the horses' mouths and making their gait far from smooth.

She was so preoccupied with his driving, on the verge once or twice of protesting his inept handling of his horses, that she failed to notice they had left Bloomsbury and, having skirted the edges of the fashionable dwellings of Mayfair, were now entering the bottom of St. James's Street. Mr. Walker chose that moment to slow his horses to a walk. It was not until they were passing a number of houses with bow-fronted windows that she realized where they were. Gentlemen seated in the windows nudged each other as they passed and those gathered in groups on the side of the street looked at the equipage with frank curiosity. For the first time in her life, Nina wished she were not driving alone with a man. All eyes seemed to be on her.

When they drew to a halt outside a narrow house about half way down the street, she was dumbstruck. When Mr. Walker had talked about the edges of Mayfair, she had never imagined his home would be on St. James's Street! Surely his sister would not enjoy the prospect of mingling with all these gentlemen every time she set foot out of doors. Then she remembered Maura was bedridden. Perhaps she enjoyed the sight of the throng from her windows. For this was the site of the notorious clubs where all the gentlemen of the *ton,* and those who aspired to be, spent much of their day and evening playing cards and making ridiculous wagers with their cronies for very high stakes. The only women who frequented the street, for no female could enter the hallowed portals of the Clubs themselves, were of a sort Nina, for all her outspokenness, did not care to name.

But Mr. Walker slowly descended the phaeton, made a business of handing the reins to a link boy and giving him whispered instructions, then walked around to her.

"Miss Chatterton," he said in a loud voice, and she saw a few heads turn in recognition of the name, "allow me to help you down."

She had no option than to do so. Keeping her head down, she allowed herself to be ushered towards the front door. Mr. Walker unlocked it and peremptorily pushed her inside.

Chapter Twenty-Three

Nina found herself facing a gloomy corridor, leading to a narrow staircase, with what probably were the kitchen and scullery beyond. Two doors led off the corridor on the right. The walls were bare, the paint, from what she could see in the gathering dark, chipped and discolored. The floor was covered in dirty drugget. There were no lit candles and it was completely silent. She was surprised. Mr. Walker seemed a well-set-up young man. These premises looked very poor and almost uninhabited. A faint suspicion entered her mind, then when her companion opened one of the doors and unceremoniously pushed her inside, the suspicion bloomed into a horrible certainty.

The room contained nothing but a narrow bed and a deal table on which was laid out what looked like a simple supper. There was one unlit candle. There was no window, for it was evidently the back half of a pair of salons separated by a folding door. This was closed tight and presumably locked.

She turned to Mr. Walker. "Where have you brought me? This cannot be your sister's room."

He shook his head, with a little smile. "You are right. It isn't. In fact, I have no sister. There is no one here but we two."

Nina shrank back from him, and bit her lip to stop herself from crying out. She would not have this treacherous man see she was afraid.

"You need have no fear," he said. "I shall offer you no violence. In fact, I shall offer you nothing but a bed for the night and a bite to eat – alone. But I shall lock you in. It's no use crying out. There will be no one to hear you. Be careful how you use the candle. There is only the one, and it will be very dark in here. I don't recommend trying to set a fire with it. There will be wet mattresses against the doors and you will only succeed in suffocating yourself. You see, Miss Chatterton, you should be careful who you write about in the newspapers. You will find the person whom you have so openly criticized is not the only one whose reputation suffers. I shall free you in the morning. Until then, I wish you goodnight."

"But who are you? Why are you doing this?" she cried. "I've never done anything to hurt you!"

"No, but you have injured a man who is able to pay me handsomely to avenge him. Unlike you, Miss Chatterton, I was not born with means. I have to make my way in the world as best I may."

"But I can pay you more!"

"Perhaps, but I think you would not be so implacable an enemy as the man who hired me, should I disappoint him. You had best accept your fate, have some supper and go to sleep. You will find the sheets clean and aired. I shall not harm you. I'm not a barbarian."

"Is Walker your real name?"

He shrugged. "I'm afraid not, nor am I remotely interested in animals. I'm sorry to disappoint you. But you did make a very fine speech, I'll give you that."

"My friends will find out who you are and make you pay!" said Nina, her teeth gritted.

"I fear your friends may not wish to be involved with you after they find out you have spent the night with a man to whom you are neither married nor betrothed, and have flaunted it for all of St. James's Street to see."

He opened the door, closed it behind him and she heard the key turn in the lock.

Nina sank onto the bed and tears came to her eyes. She angrily brushed them away. It was her own fault. She hadn't listened to Elliott when he said she should be careful dealing with a man like Parsons. She had not listened to her grandmother or Mitchell when they said she should not go around town alone. She never listened to anyone. What a fool she was!

She took off her bonnet and lay back on the pillows. She passed the whole history of the last few months in her mind. She should never have agreed to have a coming-out. She had been perfectly happy with her parents in the country. It was only the fight to ensure passage of the Animal Rights Bill that had brought her to London, and when that was accomplished, she should have gone home. It would have disappointed her grandmother, but she would have avoided the whole entanglement with Lord Devin and the Colonel. She wished she had never met either of them. Knowing Elliott Devin had brought her nothing but heartache, and she knew she shouldn't have accepted the Colonel's offer. She could never love him and the prospect of spending her life with a man she didn't care for, while seeing the one she really loved with her best friend, was unbearable.

But that, at least, would be over now. She knew her captor was right. The news of her having been seen going into a house with a single man and not emerging till the morning would rage around a gossip-hungry London in a moment. She would be a fallen woman. She was sure Mitchell would no longer want to marry her. He had said he wanted a lady to be the mother of his children. He wouldn't want a woman of no reputation. He was too conservative for that. She would go back to her grandmother's, write a letter to the Colonel releasing him from their engagement, and go home. Her parents would be disappointed in her, but they would not turn their backs on her, and she was sure that after a while her grandmother would come around. And she would never see Devin again.

She sighed and sat up. Now that was settled, she felt quite calm. In fact, she was even hungry. She had eaten very little lunch, being occupied polishing her speech. It was really quite dark now. She lit the candle with the tinder box left for the purpose and could see what her captor had provided for supper. There was bread and cheese, an open bottle of wine with a glass, and an apple. There was a plain wooden chair by the table and she sat down. She broke off a piece of the bread and chewed it. She nibbled at the cheese. Though she rarely drank alcohol, she shrugged and poured out a glass of the wine. She sipped at it, consuming more of the bread and cheese. It was really quite good.

She almost laughed. If she had been the heroine of one of the novels she read with her friends at school, she would be tearing her hair in despair. A dashing hero would be coming to her rescue. She would certainly be too overcome to sit and enjoy her supper. Or perhaps she would have attacked her captor with a broken bottle and fought her way out. To confront the crowd on St. James's Street in a blood-covered gown and be brought before the magistrate for attempted murder? No, real life was not like that. No hero came to rescue you from your own folly; you did get hungry even when you were held captive; and you didn't turn into a murderer just because your reputation was in tatters. She finished her bread and cheese, drank another glass of wine and crunched the apple. Then she picked up the candle and took it with her over to the bed. She did not feel in any danger from her captor, she was full of bread and cheese and slightly hazy from the wine. She lay down, snuffed the candle and in a little while fell asleep. It had been a long day.

She didn't know what time it was when she was awoken by the grating of the key in the lock. She immediately sat up. Her head felt like a block of wood and her throat was very dry. She felt awful. "Walker" came in carrying a teapot with a cup, saucer and a plate of something which he placed on the table.

"I thought you'd like some tea and a piece of bread and butter," he said.

"Oh, tea! Yes I would!" And force of habit made her say, "Thank you."

"Then I shall leave you to enjoy it and return in a little while."

"What time is it?"

"It is close to ten o'clock."

"Goodness! I slept a long time."

"I'm glad you were comfortable," said her captor with a wry smile, and left the room, locking the door behind him.

Nine stood up on unaccountably shaky legs and went to the table. She sat down, poured herself a cup of steaming tea and drank it, scalding as it was. Then she poured another. By the time she had finished she found her head was much clearer, and she could face the bread and butter.

"And the condemned enjoyed a hearty breakfast," she muttered as she finished the last of it.

Her hair had partly fallen from its pins overnight. "I must look a fright!" she said to herself, then took out the rest of the pins and massaged her scalp. How wonderful it felt! For the first time in her life she wished she were like other girls of her acquaintance who carried a small mirror and comb in her reticule, which she still had with her. But hers contained the tool for removing horses' shoes and a jar of salve for their wounds. Neither was much use in her present predicament, so she simply ran her fingers through her hair and braided it back. Then she picked up her hat from where it lay on the floor and fixed it on as best she could. After a night of supposed dissipation, she thought she might be expected to look somewhat disheveled.

When "Walker" returned, she was ready. She followed him, head erect, as he opened the front door and stepped into the street. There were already people about, mostly men. Some peep o' day boys might just be heading home, while others who had more regular hours were strolling to the clubs for a drink before luncheon. The gaudy carriage was standing there.

"Thank you, but I shall take a hackney," said Nina.

"If you wish to wait on the side of the street until one arrives, certainly," replied her escort. "But hackneys are not always happy to pick up the… er, women of a certain type who tend to loiter in St. James's Street. You will be quicker removed from this place if you allow me to drive you."

Nina hesitated but saw the sense in what he said. She was helped into the phaeton and once more passed beneath the gaze of men in those bow windows.

"I take it this is not your carriage?" she said to her companion.

"No, it belongs to the, er… gentleman who recruited me."

"I thought as much," she replied. "It's of a piece with the rest of his belongings: tasteless and gaudy. Besides, you are a remarkably ham-fisted driver."

"I told Mr…, er, *him* I was not much of an expert in driving a phaeton and pair, but he would have it."

"It certainly is memorable," replied Nina tartly. "And I suppose those were not your lodgings?"

"No, they were rented for the purpose." Her companion looked rather shamefaced.

"Then I must thank you for providing for me so... admirably. I don't suppose that was part of the deal."

"I had no orders concerning that, but I did not want you to be uncomfortable." He hesitated then continued. "I must say, I admire you, Miss Chatterton. Another woman might have had a fit of the vapors, or fainted, or hammered on the doors all night. As far as I can tell, you ate your supper and went to bed."

"Yes. I realized there was nothing I could do, so it was useless crying about it. In any case, you may have perhaps solved a problem for me." She laughed a little bitterly. "Perhaps I should be thanking you."

Her companion looked mystified, but they had by now reached the bottom of the street where her grandmother lived. "I wish you would let me off here," said Nina. "I have no desire for the butler to see you, or this monstrosity of a carriage."

When the horses drew to a halt, she leaped nimbly down and without looking back, strode off down the street.

Mr. James Smith, Esquire looked after her, shaking his head in wonder. "What a woman!" he said, before inexpertly turning his carriage around and setting out for St. George's Street.

Chapter Twenty-Four

Nina did exactly as she had planned. She shook her head at the elderly butler who told her that her grandmother had been sleepless all night worrying about where she was. They had sent a note to Miss Underwood, but she had been unable to throw any light on it, and finally the old lady had taken a cachet and fallen asleep. He did not like to wake her now, but Miss would be able to explain it all later.

"I am leaving for home immediately," she said. "You will please have my maid bring me up hot water and come to help me change. Then she can pack my things and send them on. I shall take the Stage from Holborn this afternoon."

As he began to protest, she added. "It's for the best, you'll see. Grandmother will understand. I'll write her a note."

And with that, she ran upstairs. She sat at her desk and wrote first to the Colonel, then to her grandmother. The latter missive ran:

Dear Grandmother,
You will be hearing the dreadful news that I spent the night with a man, not the Colonel, and that many people saw me in his company on St. James's Street. It is true that I spent the night in his house, but I did not go willingly. It was a plot to ruin my reputation. You must believe me when I say I did nothing wrong. But the

world will think I did, and I cannot prove otherwise. It is best for me to leave at once, so that you may say, truthfully, you know nothing more about it.
I am releasing Colonel Gaynor from our betrothal because he will not want to marry me when he finds out what I am accused of. I shall see about sending a letter to the newspapers announcing the end of the engagement.
I know I have been an unsatisfactory granddaughter, and you have always wished better for me. But I shall be happy at home with Mama and Papa and the animals. You are the kindest and best grandmother anyone could have, and I'm sorry to have let you down. I hope you will forgive me one day.
Your most affectionate granddaughter,
Wilhelmina

The letter to the Colonel was, curiously, easier to write. She knew he did not really love her. He would be disappointed, but she was persuaded he would find another, and more suitable, wife.

Agog with curiosity, her maid came up to help her change. Nina revealed nothing and quite sharply told her to simply pack her bags and have them sent on.

In under an hour, she was on the way to Holborn. The Stage would take her to Welwyn in Hertfordshire, the closest village to her home. She was known there and would easily get a ride to her parents' estate.

The effect on her grandmother when she awoke and was told that Nina had come home and left almost immediately, was all that one might have expected. When she read her letter, she shrieked, fell back on her pillows and fainted clean away. This was unfortunate, as before waving the vinaigrette under her nose, her nosy dresser picked the letter from her limp grasp and quickly understood its contents. In no time the news was all over the household. Nina's maid declared that she would not serve a fallen woman, and refused to continue packing her clothes. The housekeeper, who instantly saw in Nina a woman like herself, disappointed in love and left to make her own way in the world, told the maid to do as she was told or leave the house immediately. This brought on a fit of the vapors in the younger woman, and the impressionable downstairs and kitchen maids, fed on a diet of gothic romances from the lending libraries, stopped working altogether to gather around her in an attempt to glean the gory details. The cook, having called three times for someone to peel the potatoes for dinner, stormed out of the kitchen and raged at the world in general. The poor old butler, who for years had led a staid and even existence, did not know how to deal with any of it and shut himself away in his parlor, bringing a glass of port to his lips with a trembling hand.

It was some time before an uneasy peace was restored. Nina's grandmother finally roused herself and, clad in funereal black with a heavy veil, set forth to visit her friend Betsy Wainwright, who always knew everything before anyone else and was sure to be able to report the latest *on-dits*.

"Yes," said Betsy, shaking her head. "Miss Chatterton was seen last night entering an address on St. James Street, of all places, with a young man, and then leaving again this morning. And in a very colorful phaeton with yellow wheels! It's almost as if she was determined to be seen. I'm so sorry, my dear. But there seems no doubt."

"But in her letter Nina says it was all a plot! She swears she did nothing wrong!"

"Well, plot or not, doing wrong or not, it's all the *appearance* that counts, you know it as well as I do. I'm afraid she will no longer be welcome anywhere amongst the *ton*."

"She is well aware of that and has already left town. I just don't know what I should do! Should I deny it? Accept it? What?"

"The best thing for you is to say nothing at all. Stay out of society for the time being. Go away on holiday, perhaps. With both you and Nina gone, there will be no one to feed the gossip and it will all die down. By next season everyone will have forgotten all about it."

"*Next season*?" cried her visitor aghast. "You mean I shall have to stay hidden for the rest of this one? Oh, that I should get to my age and be a pariah! It's really too bad of Wilhelmina!" She burst into tears.

Hermione Underwood heard of the disaster almost immediately, but refused to believe it. Her aunt received a note on the very morning of the affair from one of her friends who kept her finger on the pulse of the *ton*. She and her niece were enjoying breakfast when it arrived. She scanned the note and gasped, opening and closing her mouth like a fish out of water, till even her habitually placid niece was forced to ask what the matter was.

"Miss Chatterton," she gasped. "Seen with a man *in flagrante delicto*!"

"Whatever can you mean, Aunt?"

"On St. James's Street," came the strangled reply.

"Nonsense!" said Hermione. She took the note from her aunt's limp grasp and read it. "I don't believe it," she declared. "Nina is a little careless but she would never do such a thing. Never."

It wasn't until she received a visit from the Colonel later in the day that she was forced to accept that her friend had done the worst thing an unmarried girl could do.

Away in Basildon, the Colonel had known nothing of the affair until he came home and found Nina's letter on his mantlepiece. He read it, uttered an oath and dropped to a chair, with his head in his hands.

Dear Mitchell,
I am writing to release you from our betrothal for the reason you may have already heard about.
If you have heard I was seen entering a home in the company of a young man and not leaving till this morning, it is true. It all happened on St. James's Street and many people saw me, so it is useless to deny it. Please believe me when I say I was the victim of a deliberate trap to ruin me. I will say no more as I don't wish you to involve yourself in this sorry affair. Rest assured I suffered no bodily harm.

Dear Mitchell, I know this will come as a heavy blow, but in your heart you will know it is for the best. You do not love me, and you also know that while I respect and like you, my heart is not engaged either. When you offered for me you told me you wanted a lady as wife and mother to your children. I can no longer fill that function, so I am no good to you. We would end up hating and blaming each other. You will find another wife who will truly love you. You are a good man and you deserve that.

I am going back to my parents in the country. An appropriate notice will appear in the papers. Please do not come after me or attempt to persuade me from an action that, in the end, will prove to have saved us from a marriage that would bring joy to neither of us.

I'm very sorry for the unpleasantness you will certainly have to endure at the hands of the gossips and so-called friends. I wish I could shield you from it.

Please show this letter to Hermione. I don't have time to write to her now, but she is the best of my friends and will do doubt have to endure innuendo and criticism because of it. I deeply regret it. I hope you will be able to support each other.

I must ask you both, please, not to write to me for the time being. I need to get away from everything to do with London, even you, my dear friends. I hope you understand.

Your friend forever,
Wilhelmina Chatterton

When he showed the letter to Hermione, all the color drained from her face. "Poor, poor girl," she cried. "Oh Nina! How many times have I earnestly told her to be careful! I knew her passion and enthusiasm would get her into trouble one day. I am so sorry for her! But what can I do?"

"What can either of us do?" he responded, "other than refuse to listen to gossip about her and continue to believe in her good name. She tells me not to follow her, and even if I did, what good would it be? She doesn't want me involved. And what she says is true. Marriage between us now would be folly. Hermione, my dear! It's you I love. I think perhaps Nina knows it too."

"And I love you," said Hermione softly. Then, falling against his broad chest, "Oh, Mitchell, it is wicked, but I can't help rejoicing at this turn of events." She turned brimming eyes up at him. "You will be free!"

Chapter Twenty-Five

Elliott Devin had left London to accompany his mother home on the morning of Nina's talk to the Animal Rights Committee. He stayed at Uplands ten days dealing with the affairs of the estate, and consequently heard nothing of Nina's disgrace. The first he knew of it was when he strolled into his club on the evening of his return to the capital and ran into his friend Marius. They played a few hands of piquet and drank a glass of two of port.

"So, what have I missed since I've been away?" asked Elliott, not with any great interest, it must be said, for he rarely allowed any gossip amongst his peers to ruffle his calm.

"Not much," said Marius. "Wait a minute though! That business with your fiancée's bosom bow? Miss Chatterton. D'you hear about that?"

"No, what about her?" replied Elliott, his voice still perfectly even, though his heart gave a sudden jolt.

"Left town in shame. Reputation ruined and all that. Something about a man and St. James's Street. Had to be about the time you left, I think."

Elliott had to exercise all his self-control not to exclaim. But all he said was, "Really? How odd!" He handed the cards to Marius, saying calmly. "Your deal."

His mind working furiously, he first thought what he'd heard was impossible. Then he realized it was not. She was so trusting. She could not have willingly done whatever she was accused of, but she could easily have made herself a prey to someone who wished to injure her. His mind went immediately to what she had told him about pursuing the owner of most of the hackneys in London. And that letter in the newspapers. He had warned her.

He gently prompted Marius for details, but he was not able to tell him much more. In fact, with no one to keep the flames fanned, the story was already beginning to fade. This was helped by the fact that the King, having lost his albeit unloved Queen only a little over a year before, now seemed to have given up any pretense of mourning and was openly and scandalously consorting with a variety of young women at his palace down in Brighton. His exploits filled the papers. Elliott ended the evening not much better informed but, as he walked home, he was determined to get to the bottom of the story.

He learned a little more the following morning when he received a visit from his betrothed. He was in the drawing room, Horace as usual on his knee. He had taken the cat with him to Uplands, hoping to be able to leave him there with his mother, and fearing wholesale departure of his staff in London if they were forced to stay for several days with a wailing cat. Horace arched his back when Hermione came into the room, but as he put him down and rose to his feet, Elliott firmly rebuked him and the cat remained quiet.

For once, his fiancée was not accompanied by her maid. Hermione had decided she must break off her engagement with his lordship, and wanted no witnesses. Mitchell Gaynor had been a frequent visitor to her aunt's and she thought the staff must be beginning to suspect something. There was no need to give them further ammunition just yet.

Almost before she had a chance to settle herself, much less say why she had come, Elliott asked lightly, "What's this I hear about our friend Miss Chatterton? It cannot be true she's gone away with her reputation in tatters."

"I'm afraid it is," replied Hermione, glad of something to start the conversation. "She was seen by a number of reliable witnesses willingly entering the man's house and not leaving till the following morning. I wish it were not so, but there can be no doubt about it."

"But there must be doubt as to why she did it. She would never have done such a thing without good reason."

"I agree, but when she wrote to the Colonel breaking off their engagement, she gave no details and said she wanted no one to follow her. He went to the address in St. James's Street but could find out nothing. It had been rented by letter. The owner never saw the man and the name given – a Mr. Walker – was untraceable. We have been able to do nothing except refuse to listen to the gossip. It has been quite dreadful."

"She has broken off her engagement?" Elliott could not prevent himself from seizing on this piece of information.

"Yes. She said she could not keep him to it under the circumstances. She asked us not to write to her, so I have no other explanation. She simply said it was best this way.

I find her so admirable, even after all this. And... and that brings me, Elliott, to the purpose of my visit."

Lord Devin was still thinking about Nina and was only half listening. He said nothing, so Hermione carried on.

"I am here for the same purpose, I'm afraid, Elliott." Devin still said nothing. In fact, he hardly took in what she was saying, but Hermione took it as a sign he wished her to continue.

She took a deep breath. "I cannot marry you. We should not suit. You have about you a laziness and an inclination to not take things seriously that would, I think, cause a rift between us. You are inclined to joke where I am of a more serious disposition. And then there is the question of the cat."

"Horace," interjected Elliott softly. He had finally become aware of what Hermione was about. "His name is Horace. I think you know that, my dear."

"Yes, well then, there is the question of Horace. I said at the ball I would not return to this house while he was still here, yet here he still is. It is precisely this type of inaction I was referring to."

"Yes, here he still is. But you know, my dear, I took him to Uplands with every intention of leaving him with my mother. However, if I was absent for more than a couple of hours, he acted as though I had abandoned him. Mama said she could not bear the wailing."

"And that was more important to you than my being able to live here?"

"Well, it was more important to my mother," he replied with a smile. "Living with a creature who wails like the damned in hell is not conducive to domestic tranquility."

Hermione's voice rose. "There you are: you simply smile at the problem! But for me, too, living with a creature who hisses and claws and clearly expresses his dislike is not conducive to it either!"

Recalling Nina's words, Elliott replied, "perhaps he remembers when you first met you tried to have him drowned. A thing like that is hard to get over, I'm sure you agree. But I thought perhaps you could learn to like him a little, then he might learn to like you… a little."

"I'm sorry to disappoint you, Elliott, but I have no intention of trying to get the cat… Horace to like me. In fact, it would have been better for both of us had he been drowned."

"But not better for him," his lordship's ready smile came to his lips.

"Really, Elliott! Again! You have about you a quirk for taking things much more lightly than you should. It is a characteristic I cannot like."

She waited, but when he said nothing, took off the engagement ring he had given her, and tried to hand it back.

Elliott shook his head. "No, Hermione. Keep the ring. You deserve it for putting up with me – and Horace – as long as you have. It can become no one as well as it becomes you. Keep it in a spirit of friendship. I sincerely hope we shall remain friends."

She made as if to protest, but he gently closed her fingers around the ring. She hesitated, then put it in her reticule. "Thank you," she said.

"You know, Hermione," he said, smiling, "I think we shall like each other much better now."

"You may be right." This time she smiled back.

They both stood. Hermione took his proffered arm and they walked towards the door.

Horace, who had leaped into his lordship's chair, regarded them both with satisfaction. He had done well, he thought.

Chapter Twenty-Six

Coming back into the drawing room, Elliott pushed Horace off his chair and sat down. Horace, miffed at the treatment, went off to see if the study door was open. He fancied a game of dominoes. But the maids, tired of finding the tiles scattered all over the floor, were now careful to shut the door. So he padded silently back to the drawing room where his master sat, deep in thought. He jumped on his knee and provided what he considered the invaluable service of a back for him to stroke while he was thinking.

That was just what Elliott needed, apparently, for a few minutes later he rang the bell for Minton.

"Tell that boy – what was his name? Dick – from the stables, to come and see me."

His lordship spoke in his usual languid manner, and there was no hint in his voice that he had come to several important decisions. Nevertheless, the request was so unusual that Minton blinked. But all he said was, "At once, my lord."

Dick arrived about ten minutes later. He was an unprepossessing youth with a thin face and a body like a coiled spring. But the light of intelligence shone from his eyes. He had evidently tried to clean himself up for the interview. His coarse hair had been plastered down with water, though a few recalcitrant strands were still sticking straight up, and he had washed the hands now damply grasping the cap he was turning around and around in them.

"You're a bright lad," said his lordship. "I want you to find out something for me. Quietly. No blabbing it around the stables or to your friends when you have a jar of an evening. Understood?"

"Yessir," replied Dick fervently. He would do anything for the master who had supported him over the Champion affair. Old Turner, the head groom, hadn't dared say a word to him afterwards, though the atmosphere in the stables continued to be strained.

Lord Devin explained what he wanted, gave the boy several coins saying to use them as he saw fit, and sent him off.

A few hours later Dick was lounging around the stables in the mews behind Nina's grandmother's townhouse.

"Might be lookin' fer a new position," he said to Timothy, the old groom who presided over the establishment. "I'm wiv a Lord at the moment but the hours is dreadful. 'E's out till all hours an' then I'm 'avin' to wake up to deal wiv the 'orses. I needs me sleep. I bet yer don't have nothin' like that 'ere, with the old lady."

"It's not fer me to gabble 'bout 'er ladyship's 'abits," responded the old groom, his eye nonetheless caught by the glint of a coin in the boy's hand.

"Nah, course not," replied Dick. "But it's thirsty work, innit? Me dad always tole me yer gets nuffin' fer nuffin'. I'd stand yer a pint if yer willin'."

So it was that a little while later they were head-to-head in the local pub, and Timothy was telling him that her ladyship always had very regular habits indeed, and these days was not venturing out at all, being as there had been a to-do with her granddaughter what used to be staying there.

"In trouble, was she? She go anywhere a bit... well, yer knows, a bit off, like, while she were 'ere?" asked Dick casually.

"Only that one time, to St. George's Street – number 30 it were. Not eckzackly a bad 'ouse, but not where we was used to go. I was never there before nor since."

Since this was exactly one of the pieces of information Lord Devin had asked him to find out, Dick paid for another round, said he'd be back if conditions in his present employment got any worse, and took himself off to the mews of number 30 St. George's Street.

His job here promised to be a little more difficult, since his lordship had told him to find out as much as he could about the homeowner and everywhere he went. However, the groom here, a sour, miserable-looking creature who had no fondness for his tight-fisted master, would have opened his soul to Dick even without the pie and pint he was offered.

"Yuss," he said, taking a large bite of the pie and masticating it slowly, "Old Parsons, 'e don't mind having me an' the 'orses standin' about in all wevvers. Only reason I ain't wiv 'im this mornin' is acoz he took Jem instead. Said me liv'ry needed cleanin'! Liv'ry! Clown outfit more like! Yeller and red like 'is carriage!"

It transpired that apart from the morning and evening visits to the stables over Charing Cross way, Mr. Parsons' most frequent destination was his club, the Pen and Paper on Old Queen Street, not far from St. James's Park. Then there was his solicitor at Throgmortons, he thought it was called. He'd been there a few times.

Dick hurried back to Devin House and conveyed all this intelligence to Lord Devin. Elliott thanked him warmly, gave him a sovereign and sent him back to the stables. Dick went with a spring in his step, thinking he would treat his best girl to a slap-up supper that evening. Who knew how she might repay him?

In his study, Elliott started to write a note to the Devin family solicitors asking if they knew of the firm of Throgmortons and where they might be found. Horace, who had jumped up on his desk hoping for a game of dominoes, found the movement of his lordship's pen very interesting. Wanting to help with the composition of the note, he leaped upon it, causing the nib to splutter ink everywhere. He then padded onto the ivory paper with his inky paws.

Elliott cursed, then spoke to his assistant. "Horace! when I need your help in composing a note, I'll ask for it. Kindly remove your feet from my writing paper and your nose from the nib of my pen. Unless you wish to mend it for me? No, I thought not. Mind your own business and let me mind mine!"

Horace removed himself to the edge of the wide desk and began cleaning his paws and whiskers. Elliott started his note again and soon both accomplished their tasks, each to his own satisfaction. His lordship folded his missive, sealed it by pressing the face of his signet ring into a blob of hot wax on the flap, and walked into the hall to give it to Minton. Horace followed not more than six inches from his boots.

"Please see that this note is delivered as soon as may be," he said to the butler. "I expect the footman can wait for the answer. Meanwhile I'm going to my club. Try to keep Horace out of the study, if you can. He has moved from playing dominoes to wanting to become a scribe, but his use of ink is a little uncontrolled."

Prevented from following his master into the street, Horace slunk down into the kitchens. He curled up in his basket by the fire in which lay one of his lordship's old waistcoats. Not even a piece of succulent rabbit saved from the staff's dinner could tempt him out. He sniffed at it contemptuously and turned his head away.

The reply to his lordship's note was waiting for him when he returned from his club later that afternoon. He read it in the hall, asked Minton to call his carriage and told Horace, who, as usual, knew when his god was back in the house even before he said a word, and was now curling around his boots in welcome, that he was sorry, but he was going out again.

"I know, I know," he said. "I deplore the need for activity as much as you do, but I think you will find it in a good cause. I'll tell you all about it later."

Not long afterwards, his lordship's curricle was standing before the door of Throgmorton and Throgmorton, Solicitors. It was in a solid, reliable-looking building though not in the most prosperous location. Leaving the groom to walk the horses, he entered the premises and handed his card to a bowing lackey who, before he even read it, recognized the quality of the card and the impeccable tailoring of its owner. When he saw the name on the card, he stood up straighter and bowed lower. He asked the visitor to sit for a moment and scurried off to find one of the partners.

Mr. Throgmorton Senior appeared several minutes later and was profusely apologizing for keeping the noble visitor waiting when Lord Devin gently interrupted the flow to say, "I should like an interview with the person who handles Mr. Parsons' affairs. He did tell me the name, but I'm afraid, my memory…"

He tailed off, leaving Mr. Throgmorton to fill in the gap with, "Ah yes, Mr. Smith. Our young colleague. But perhaps I or my brother could…"

"Thank you, but I particularly wish to see Mr. Smith. He acted for Mr. Parsons on a matter of some delicacy, I believe."

Mr. Throgmorton understood. A delicate matter. Probably dealing with an opera-singer or some such, he surmised. Lord Devin would not want his family solicitors handling such things. Much better an unknown like young James Smith.

"Certainly, my lord. Follow me, if you please."

Elliott was led into a small office containing not much more than a somewhat beaten desk and a rather good-looking man perhaps a couple of years younger than he, who leaped to his feet. Mr. Throgmorton presented his lordship to Mr. James Smith, Esquire, begged him to be seated and bowed himself out.

James had no idea what Lord Devin could want with him until, to his horror, he heard, "I understand you recently took a lease on a premises in St. James's Street under the name of Walker and on behalf of Mr. Albert Parsons."

"Sir, I don't..." he spluttered.

"Let us not waste time with denials, Mr. Smith," said his lordship, his languid demeanor gone. He had guessed Parsons would employ an unknown solicitor to rent the premises and they would use a false name. "We both know what I say is correct. Our business will be so much sooner concluded if we can just move on. Allow me to continue. I also understand that Mr. Parsons is a member of a club called the Pen and Paper on Old Queen Street. Since it's known as a club for persons of your profession, it's my belief you must have introduced him there."

He looked the other man steadily straight in the eyes.

"Er, yes," replied Smith looking down. He found he could not lie to this stranger with the piercing gaze. "I acted for him in the purchase of his house on St. George's Street and as it was clear he wanted to, er, move up in the world, I proposed him for membership of my club."

"Well, I wish you to propose me, too."

Mr. Smith goggled. "You want to become a member of The Pen and Paper Club?"

His head was spinning. First this lord of the realm had come into his office apparently knowing all his business and now he wanted to join his club. Why? He was surely a member of all the *ton* clubs Smith himself could only aspire to.

"Yes, and I wish you to present me to Mr. Parsons. I understand he's a most, er, enterprising fellow. I assume you have a card room. Tell me, what games does he prefer?"

"I, er... he's not much one for cards, sir, but he does enjoy throwing the dice. And he seems lucky with them. He is often at the dice table in the evenings."

"Good. You will take me to the club and introduce me to the dice table. It will be as if by chance. You will not tell him I know of his involvement in the St. James's Street... débacle, nor that I have come specially to meet him. If he should ask how you know me, you may say your father knew mine and recommended you to me. Let us say the day after tomorrow at nine o'clock. I leave it to you to make sure Mr. Parsons is there."

Mr. Smith simply nodded, dumbly.

Lord Devin rose. "I will not shake your hand, Mr. Smith," he said. "Your cowardly actions in destroying the reputation of an innocent young woman have taken away any right you had to be treated as a gentleman. I shall for now say nothing to anyone about what I have discovered, but should I hear at any time that you have attempted to move into that level of society for which being a gentleman is a necessary prerequisite, I shall speak up. I'm sure you understand me."

He had spoken quietly and without any particular emphasis. But there was no denying the steel in his voice, nor his cold, hard look as he looked straight into James

Smith's eyes. The younger man flushed and dropped his gaze. He understood. He had regretted his lies to Miss Chatterton almost as soon as he uttered them, and he had meant what he said when he left her. She was an admirable woman. In destroying her, he knew now that he had destroyed himself and all his hopes for the future. He cursed the day he had met Albert Parsons.

Chapter Twenty-Seven

Elliott Devin was only half an hour late to the Pen and Paper Club, a promptness that would have astounded those who knew him. He entered the rather dark premises and Mr. Smith, who had been on thorns awaiting his arrival, hurried forward to meet him, not looking him in the eye or offering to shake his hand, instead bowing rather formally.

"Lord Devin is my guest," he announced to the membership secretary, who stood guard at the desk. "He wishes to have a look round before applying for membership."

"Most certainly, sir," the secretary bustled forward, delighted to welcome a Peer into the premises. He was the sort of member one wanted, not East End tradesmen made good. "Please let me know if I may furnish you with any additional information."

Elliott followed Mr. Smith into a comfortable parlor room where gentlemen were sitting in groups, reading the newspapers or chatting, most often with a glass at their elbow. From there he was led into the much larger games room, brilliantly lit, where men sat at different tables playing various card games. Amongst them he could discern Whist, Faro and Bézique. As far as he could tell, there was no Basset, not surprisingly, since a great deal of money could be lost at the game, and he doubted these gentlemen had the means required. Solicitors were not, on the whole, a wealthy group. In one corner there was a table where the rattling of dice could be heard.

"Our mutual er, friend, is at the dice table," murmured Mr. Smith in the visitor's ear.

"Then let us join him," replied Elliott, and allowed himself to be led in the direction of the rattling.

They waited for a moment while a player rolled his dice, ending up losing. Then, as the dice were being passed to the next man, Mr. Smith spoke up.

"Gentlemen, allow me to present Lord Devin. He is visiting this evening and, er, may become a member."

There was a murmur of approval as the players half stood, each giving his name and a nod. Elliott noted that the man with the bushy side whiskers and practically bald pate was Albert Parsons.

"May I join you, gentlemen?" he asked with his engaging smile. "I confess to being fond of the dice, though I cannot say the dice are often fond of me!"

There was a polite titter of laughter and more than one breast was stirred by the idea of winning from a Lord. He was welcomed with open arms.

In truth, Elliott rarely played dice. He preferred something where he had at least a modicum of control over the outcome. But he cheerfully added his pound note (low stakes, he noted, just as he had thought) to the pile in the center of the table and watched it being swept away by a man who rolled a 7 on his first throw. The dice passed around, Mr. Parsons coming next. He blew on the dice in the leather cup, he tapped his knuckles on the table. It was obvious that here was a man whose habits had been formed over years of playing. Finally he threw – a three. Automatic loss. He sighed and passed the dice. At last it was Elliott's turn. He had by now lost money without throwing once. But he had no desire to win. He wanted his new friends to think him a good and ready loser. He shook the cup, threw the dice and lost. He shrugged and passed on the dice with a rueful smile. When, after his usual performance, Mr. Parsons played again, he threw an 11 and won on his first round. He looked around in triumph.

"I would drink to your continued success, Mr. Parsons," said Elliott, but I daresay as a non-member I am not permitted to buy a round."

"Allow me, Lord Devin," Parsons said. His unusual generosity was occasioned by the glow he felt, dicing at the same table as a Peer. He was moving up in the world, and no mistake. He suddenly had a vision of his late wife. How proud she would have been! Though she herself was awkward and tongue-tied in more elevated company than she was used to, she was always proud of him.

After that, several other players bought rounds for the table, and it became very convivial indeed. The evening ended with more than one member shaking his lordship by the hand and promising support in his membership application. The result was that instead of waiting till the end of the month, there was a special meeting of the membership committee to confirm the acceptance of Lord Elliott Devin into the Pen and Paper Club.

Over the next few weeks, his lordship appeared regularly at his new club. He lunched and dined there several times and found the food rather better than at

Brook's or White's. This was, he discovered, because the members were much more inclined to complain. The concept of value for money was not one that entered the minds of most of the gentlemen of the *ton*. But when he discovered that Mr. Parsons never ate there, he confined himself to evenings in the games room, where he became a frequent participant at the dice table.

It was true that Parsons was lucky with the game. He rarely left the table a loser. Elliott would exclaim at his new friend's good fortune every time he won and offer him a congratulatory drink, or, more often buy a round for the table. So though his success was not really much more than anyone else's, little by little, it was noticed by the other players, too, some with exclamation, and some with grumbling. One day, Elliott declared with a laugh that he was going to sit on Parsons' right, in the hope of catching a winning throw before it got to him. From then on he did so, through frequently drawing attention to his own losses, even in that favored position.

A month or so went by and then one day his lordship caught up with his old friend Marius at Brooke's.

"Haven't seen you here recently, old chap," said his friend. "I thought you must be rusticating after Miss Underwood's announcement calling off your betrothal."

"What? Er... well, you know..." In fact, Elliott had hardly paid any heed to the notice in the papers and he was surprised to be reminded of it now.

"Pity," said his friend. "She's a fine-looking girl. Don't want to rub it in, but I hear she's seeing a lot of that Colonel Gaynor these days. 'Course, Miss Chatterton called off her engagement to *him* after all that business on St. James's Street. Had to. And no one's seen her since."

"Look, Marius, I don't want to talk about it," said Elliott. The mention of Nina was making him angry, and he was glad to be able to play the jilted lover to cover it up.

"Certainly, old chap," Marius commiserated. "Not another word."

There was a hesitation, then Elliott said, "Isn't one of your many unsavory friends a fellow who makes loaded dice? I seem to remember you told me that once."

"Yes! Fellow by the name of Higgins. Haven't seen him in an age. Probably deported to the Antipodes by now."

"So you don't know how I can get hold of him?"

"Why? You in the market for loaded dice?"

"As a matter of fact, yes."

"You're not going to use them in the clubs?" Marius was horrified. "And don't think about it in the Sluices either. They'll kill you and your body will never be found."

"Of course not. I want them for... well, just for a joke."

"Well then, you don't need Higgins. I've got some I can give you. Sort of thing one acquires, you know." Marius looked a little shamefaced. "Never used 'em, of course."

Elliott smiled at his friend. "A half-dozen bottles of my port for your dice," he said.

"By God, you're on!" cried Marius. "You're most definitely on!"

Chapter Twenty-Eight

A few evenings later, by prior arrangement Lord Devin met Mr. Smith earlier than usual at the Pen and Paper Club. They sat together for a few minutes while Elliott told him what he wanted him to do. The younger man looked unhappy but nodded.

In the game room the dicing had not yet begun, so Elliott sat and waited. Parsons arrived soon after and by what was now habit, sat to Elliott's left. He called one of the waiters to bring the cup and dice. A few other men came to the table, and the game began. It progressed as usual until the leather cup arrived at Elliott. He played and lost, then, as he passed the dice to Parsons remarked, "It seems unusually crowded here this evening, or am I imagining things?" As the other players looked around, he dropped the loaded dice he had been concealing in his long fingers into the cup. Parsons took it, shook, and threw a four and a three – a seven. Elliott was exclaiming at his good fortune when Mr. Smith, who had staggered over to watch the game, apparently the worse for wear, jostled the table. In the confusion, Elliott replaced the loaded dice with the true ones. Mr. Smith made an inarticulate apology and sat down to watch. The game continued. When the cup came around to him again, Elliott held his breath and played, hoping to lose again. He did.

"It's no good, Parsons," he said to his neighbor, loud enough for all the table to hear. "Your luck never seems to rub off on me. I need a drink to drown my sorrows. I hope you will all join me."

He called over the waiter and signaled to the others to place their orders and while they were thus distracted, once again replaced the true dice with the loaded ones. Parsons waited for the drinks to arrive and threw again. Another seven – a four and a three. There was a mixed murmur of congratulations and disbelief at the table. Ignoring it, a smiling Parsons rose to pull the pile of banknotes towards himself, and under the pretense of moving his drink out of the way, Elliott slipped the true dice into Parsons' pocket. Then, when Parsons went to pick up the dice to pass to the next player, James Smith suddenly said in a carrying voice, "Wait a minute!" He took the dice from Parsons' hand and threw them willy-nilly onto the table. A four and a three. He did it again, a four and a three. "These dice are loaded!" he exclaimed. "I thought there was something odd about them! Look!" He threw twice more. The dice always came up with a four and a three.

There was a general hubbub and in the midst of it, someone called, "Bring a hammer, let's break the damn things!" The Club Secretary, looking worried, came bustling over with a large hammer, and brought it down smartly upon first one dice then the other. Once they were broken open, a small piece of lead was clearly visible on the side opposite the four and the three respectively. The dice would always fall with those numbers uppermost.

There was complete and silence in the room as the other men took in the shocking implication. No one was more shocked than Mr. Parsons.

"But... but," he stammered. "I didn't, I never..."

"Mr. Parsons," broke in the Secretary, solemnly. "You, sir, are a cheat. I must ask you to empty your pockets."

He was too dumbfounded to refuse. He slowly did as he was told, first taking his stuffed billfold from his breast pocket, then placing on the table from the side pockets a rather dirty handkerchief, a couple of keys, a penknife... and two dice. The secretary picked them up and threw them. A five and a two. He threw again. A pair of fours. Those dice were clearly true. There was an uproar.

Into it, Parsons cried helplessly, "I never... it wasn't me! Must have been young Smith! He jostled the table, you remember!"

He appealed to the other men around the table and pointed a finger to where Smith was standing, swaying slightly as if still under the influence of alcohol.

"He hasn't been playing!" came one response. "He's half-cut!" came another.

"Anyway, we played a round after he sat down and we none of us threw a seven," said a third. "We must have been using the true dice then. No one else threw the loaded dice, Parsons."

"A cheat and a coward!" said someone else. "Trying to put the blame on another Member! For shame!"

"Shame! Shame! Shame!" The Secretary took Parsons firmly by the arm and propelled him out of the game room, through the parlor and into the front hall, followed by a throng of members, all chanting. "Shame! Shame! Shame!" He was thrust out into the street.

"And do not return! You are blackballed!" cried the Secretary, slamming the door behind him.

Members straggled back to their places exchanging comments, "Upstart!" "Not a gentleman!" "Remember that letter in the newspapers? The man's a cad!" "From the East End, what do you expect?"

When the Secretary came to him wringing his hands with apology and assuring him this was the first time such a thing had happened in the fifty years the club had been in existence, Elliott smiled and nodded in commiseration but said nothing. He quietly left soon after and was never seen at the Pen and Paper Club again.

Mr. Parsons stumbled down Old Queen's Street in a daze. His groom finally caught up with him and took him home in his gaudy phaeton. Of course, he knew what had happened. The drivers waiting for their masters were always the first to know everything. It wasn't long before every one of Mr. Parsons' acquaintances knew he had been caught cheating and thrown out of his club. No one was surprised or sorry for him. He had cheated and abused people his whole life.

Chapter Twenty-Nine

Parsons stayed on in his mansion on St. George's Street for a while, but the staff treated him with barely veiled contempt. He sent a note asking for an interview with Lord Devin, and was invited to attend him the following afternoon. He dressed himself carefully in his newest attire and attempted to arrange his neckcloth as his lordship did. It was not a success. When Minton opened the door into the foyer of Devin House, Parsons could see what Nina had meant. There was no ostentation here, no gilt, no large statues, no wall-sized mirrors. It was the home of a real gentleman, subdued but elegant. He was asked to wait a moment while the butler saw if his lordship was at home.

Minton trod silently into the drawing room, closed the door behind him and announced, "There is a... person desirous of seeing you, my lord. A Mr. Parsons."

He had immediately recognized that Parsons was no gentleman, in spite of his fashionable attire.

"Ah yes. Show him in, Minton, but in ten minutes interrupt to say Lord Livingston is waiting in the study."

"Of course, sir." He knew there would be no Lord Livingston.

Devin was sitting when Parsons was ushered in. He made no move to come forward or shake his visitor's hand and did not ask him to sit. Parsons was forced to remain there, rather like a schoolboy facing the headmaster, his scrawny neck poking out of an ill-tied neckcloth. Elliott seemed nothing like the friendly fellow he knew from the club. Here in his natural surroundings he was unnerving and Parsons' speech reverted to its East End origins.

"I've come, me lord," he said, hesitantly, "t'see if you knows… know anything about what 'appened t'other night at the club?"

"No," said Elliott.

"Wot I means is, did yer see anything… anything…" His voice tailed off.

"You mean did I see anyone but you handle the loaded dice?" Elliott spoke in his usual quiet fashion, though his eyes were keen and hard. "No, I did not. I rather thought the whole thing spoke for itself. It seemed clear to me, as to the others, that you had cheated."

"But I never, yer lordship!" exploded Parsons. "I mean, why would I? I wins enough and I'm… well, I'm not short of a bob. I've got no reason ter do such a thing!"

"Then I recommend you talk to the Secretary. If you lay your case before him, he might see your point."

"But that's just it, me lord, 'e won't see me! I wondered if… if you would write 'im a note, like, and…"

"I'm afraid that would not be possible. I hardly know you, Parsons. We've met a few times over the dice but I cannot vouch for your character. The only thing I could say is I noticed nothing, and I told him that on the night of the…" he hesitated, "incident."

At that moment Minton came in smoothly and announced that Lord Livingston was in the study.

Elliott stood up. "I'm sorry, Parsons, but Minton will see you out. I can't keep the Prime Minister waiting."

The visitor gulped to think he was talking to a man who had the ear of the Prime Minister. The whole visit to Devin House had been very unsettling, and he wished he had not come. He bowed awkwardly and allowed himself to be led into the hall, reunited with his hat and cane, and nodded out of the house. Minton did not bow.

A few days later Parsons received a letter from an unknown solicitor telling him he was acting for a party who wished to purchase his hackney carriage business. The sum mentioned was considerably less than he thought it might be worth, but he was so discouraged, he had no spirit for a fight. A number of those who had attended Nina's lecture were now regularly visiting his stables and taking notes. Passengers in his hackneys were still asking questions about his ownership and the people he was accustomed to nod to on St. George's Street no longer lifted their hats in response. His red and yellow phaeton was very noticeable, and he was sure observers pointed at him when he passed, telling each other about the cheating scandal. He finally knew what it was to lose what little good adhered to his name. In that respect, he had become more of a gentleman than he knew. So he accepted the low offer for his business and turned his back on fashionable London.

He sold the house on St. George's Street to a costermonger who, like him, had done well at his business. He was now the owner of several stalls in the markets of London and saw the house with all its tasteless furnishings as the height of luxury. He even kept on the servants, who saw their comfortable existence reaching far into the future. Parsons was not sad to see it go. Devin House had shown him the truth of Nina's remarks and he had begun to hate his home.

He returned to the East End where he lived the rest of his days in material comfort, surrounded by people who knew him for what he was. His money bought him friends but his sour disposition prevented him from keeping them. It also bought him a wife, a young, blowsy creature of generous proportions who led him a merry dance, spending his money as fast as she could.

He was never to know who had orchestrated the affair with the loaded dice. He never once suspected Elliott Devin, who he now thought of as so superior an individual he was amazed he'd ever met him at all. He continued to believe it was James Smith, but when he went to the firm of Throgmortons to have it out with him, he was told the young man had left. He had taken up a position in a town in the North. They didn't know where.

James Smith, Esquire had quietly left the Pen and Paper Club. The Secretary explained that it was best. He was responsible for Mr. Parsons being a member, a man whose name had been linked in the newspapers with unsavory business practices and who was then revealed to be a coward and a cheat. He had thereby brought the Club's name into disrepute and worse, it had been in the presence of Lord Elliott Devin. His lordship had not been seen since that night. A note of apology written to his address had been answered civilly but noncommittally by a secretary. It was all Mr. Smith's fault that they had lost a real gentleman through accepting a false one.

In his new position in Manchester, the young solicitor was able to leave the whole episode behind him, but he never rose to the heights of his profession he had once thought within his grasp. He spent his life making the wills of shopkeepers and widows and ended up marrying the genteel but impoverished companion of one of them. Neither fashionable nor especially handsome, she was nevertheless a good wife to him, better than he deserved, in fact. He retained his boyish good looks and she always adored him. If he strayed occasionally, she never knew, or at least, never said.

Chapter Thirty

For the second time in his life, Dick from the stables was called into his lordship's presence. He was less overawed this time, having had very satisfactory dealing with him before, and, as a consequence, even more satisfactory dealings with his best girl. They were now walking out regularly and Dick could see himself quite soon in the role of *paterfamilias*.

"I have a proposition for you, Dick," said Elliott. "It would mean leaving my stables but," as Dick began to protest, "it would be a better future for you in the end. Can you read?"

Dick assured him he could. In fact, he was an intelligent boy and in the village school where he had been educated, he had, at the end, been chiefly responsible for teaching the younger children what had come so easily to him.

"Then if you read this," continued his lordship, you will see it is a Bill of Sale transferring to me ownership of a business previously owned by a Mr. Parsons and controlling the majority of the hackney carriages in London. I do not wish this to be known and I am giving it to you now only so that you may prove you have the right to do what I wish you to do. I trust you never to mention my name."

Then he outlined what he had in mind. Dick left the study, his mind in a whirl. He went to his room above the stables and changed into his Sunday best, the suit he walked out in with his girl. "Orders of 'is lordship," he explained to the puzzled head groom Turner, and took a hackney to Charing Cross. It amused him to think of his new relationship with this vehicle and most of the others like it in the capital, but he said nothing.

Arriving at Parsons' stables, he called over the lad, not many years younger than himself, who worked there.

"I'm yer new overseer," he announced. "An' in case yer don't believe me, 'ere's the paper to prove it."

He waved the Bill of Sale in front of the lad's nose. Unlike Dick, his schooling had not been very successful and he couldn't read what he saw, but he could recognize the very official-looking stamp on it.

"Now then," continued Dick, let's 'ave a butchers at wot we got 'ere."

Dick had been long enough in London to pick up the local slang: *butcher's, short for butcher's hook* meant *look*.

He walked around with the boy, commenting unfavorably on what he saw. The horses were now routinely unharnessed and better fed, but they were still in a sorry state compared with what Dick was used to in his lordship's stables. He mentally made a list of what they would need. Lord Devin had told him to order anything he needed and have the bill sent to the solicitors whose name appeared on the Bill of Sale. He would settle with them.

Dick's mental note was extensive. To make salves: apple vinegar, spermaceti oil, lanolin, sulphur, zinc and alum; for fomenting strains and pulled muscles: a quantity of bandages. Added to this he would need several loads of clean straw, four or five brooms and hay for feed. Then there would be the materials needed to rebuild the stalls properly. The spaces that passed for stalls were divided from each other by a few pieces of splintered waste wood or rubbish. Dick had seen at once this was responsible for many of the wounds on the horses' sides.

By the time he had finished his survey, the night drivers were leading their beasts out and the day drivers were arriving. As the night horses vacated the spaces, the day drivers were leading theirs in. Men and horses had worked since six that morning and they were all tired. When he judged most of the drivers were in the yard, either coming or going, Dick climbed on top of an upturned barrel and produced a shrill whistle with his two fingers. The men's eyes all turned to him. The day horses stood, their heads down, snuffling for stray pieces of hay. The night horses stood, harnessed, patient and resigned to the long hours of work that lay ahead.

What Dick had to say astonished his audience.

"Evenin' all," he said. "My name's Dick Topper and I'm goin' to be in charge around 'ere. This business 'as been bought out. Parsons is finished. The new owner, and never you mind 'is name, is a good man. Don't go thinkin' just cuz I'm young you can pull the wool over me eyes. I've been around 'orses all me life, and worked with men too – big bully ones, like some of yer, and small mean ones like the rest. Like I jus' said, the new owner's a good man. You treat 'im right and 'e'll do the same fer you."

He took a breath, "Now, I knows I can't do it all meself. I'm goin' to need 'elp. I'm proposin' to take one of yer off the 'orses and have 'im work 'ere with me, in the yard. Collect the take mornin' and night, and work along of me fixin' up what needs doin'."

He paused again. "Yer don't know me. But yer knows each other. Now, yer just 'ave a parlay an' decide 'oo stays in the yard wiv me. He's got ter be 'onest and able ter reckon up the money. Don't yer worry, I'll be checkin' it all, an' I can reckon all right. Any mistakes will cost yer all, an' me too, so choose someone yer can trust."

Thus the almost twenty-year-old Dick Topper, who had never heard of Robert Owen and the cooperative principles of his utopian communities, created the first business in London where the workers had a share in the decision-making. When he had an idea, he put it to the men, and when he had a complaint, he did the same. He did it not out of any moral sense, but because he knew people worked best when their opinions were listened to. He had learned that from Lord Devin.

Within a couple of months the stables were cleaned and rebuilt, the horses' wounds were being treated, the carriages had been updated or replaced, and the drivers were being paid an extra guinea a week. Having for the first time in his life been put in charge of something, Dick was a veritable whirlwind. He was there first thing in the morning and often long after dark at night. He rebuilt the stalls, made up the salves for the horses, swept the straw, distributed the hay, checked the accounts. Nothing escaped him.

The man chosen by his peers to be his assistant proved to be a quiet, mousy individual who had become a hackney driver because his father had been one before him. Being bookish and shy, he had no aptitude for it and had frequently been the brunt of Parsons' wrath because he failed to bring in the money needed. The other men trusted him, however, and he proved the ideal right-hand man for Dick. He was quick with figures and enjoyed the business of ordering what was needed for the yard. He didn't particularly like horses but was willing to sweep out the stalls and generally help out. Although considerably older, he willingly took direction from the younger man and worked with a will.

Parsons' lad was at first inclined to be truculent, especially when made to work harder than before and without the bonus of the lady visitors' hay-feeding sessions. Dick welcomed the lady visitors and allowed them to feed the horses, but refused to take their money. He asked them only to spread the word that the new owner of the hackneys was a good man.

He tolerated the lad's bad humor until one morning, when he'd left instructions for a horse with a swollen leg to be wet-bandaged overnight. This was, he knew, more efficacious than dry bandaging, especially if the bandages were dipped in warm water to start. But they had to be kept wet. Drying, they would constrict the leg and do more harm than good. Dick gave the lad an extra shilling and went off to have a pie with his girl, who was complaining she never saw 'im no more. The boy always stayed in the stables overnight in a warm little den he'd made for himself. Tonight, like other nights, he simply went off to sleep and forgot the horse.

When Dick arrived early the next morning he was furious. He roused the boy from his slumber and told him if that was the best he could do, he could do it elsewhere.

"If yer ain't goin' ter do wot yer says yer will, wot good are yer? A man's got ter keep 'is word. If yer can't do that, yer no good ter me, nor ter yerself. Yer might as well sling yer hook."

The lad, conscious that he had fallen down in his duty and fearful of losing what was, after all, a good job with a very fair employer, burst into tears and begged forgiveness. It was the first time Dick had been so acutely aware he held the fate of another in his hands. A couple of the older men drivers had refused to work for him from the start, and had left. The rest had decided to see how it would work out and had stayed. The rise in earnings after the first quarter under new ownership made them pleased they had. So Dick had never had to fire anyone. He did not do so now. He patted the boy on the shoulder and told him to set about giving the horses their morning feed. Just do better next time. Joyous at this reprieve, the lad set to work and never afterwards had to be told twice to do anything.

Dick's cooperative approach paid off. He rarely had to deal with dishonest drivers, men who were cruel to their horses or people who shirked their duties. Lord Devin left him entirely in charge, merely meeting with him once a quarter. His lordship soon learned he had no need to look over the books, but listened instead to the younger man's proposals and plans. After the first quarter, Dick suggested giving the drivers, the bookkeeper and the stable lad an extra shilling a week. He would take it too, if his lordship was willing. His lordship was willing. After the third quarter, he was so willing he offered Dick a share in the profits. The younger man did not know how to respond. He pumped his employer's hand in gratitude, the words of thanks stuck in his throat.

Word got around that the hackney carriages of London were under new management. Customers noticed that the carriages were cleaner, the horses brighter and the drivers more cheerful. This culminated in a reporter from the *London Gazette* visiting the yard and writing a favorable review of what he saw. There was no mention, however, of Miss Chatterton, who had set the whole investigation in motion.

Elliott Devin was in the drawing room late the following morning, Horace on his knee, both apparently lazing as usual. In fact, his lordship had been mentally working on a problem for the past several weeks. His eyebrows went up as he saw the report in the *Gazette*, and when he also read a betrothal announcement in the Court and Society section, his mind was made up.

"Well, look at this," he said, showing the paper to Horace. "It seems our enterprise is succeeding. And Miss Chatterton's name is conspicuously absent. People really do have such short memories. And then there's this forthcoming marriage. Prepare yourself. Tomorrow we're going for a trip to the country. The foliage is turning and it should be a very pretty drive. You'll like it."

Chapter Thirty-One

The following afternoon saw Lord Devin admiring a very shapely pair of ankles emerging from serviceable boots at the top of a ladder disappearing into an apple tree. The top half of the owner of the ankles was obscured in the tree; her faded blue skirts were caught up into her waistband, so the petticoats beneath were clearly visible. Apart from the drone of bees, the drop of apples falling rhythmically into a basket was the only sound on that early autumn afternoon.

"Miss Chatterton!" he said. "How nice to see, well, as much of you as I can."

"Lord Devin!" gasped the ankle-owner. She turned abruptly and, ducking below the branches, beheld Elliott, neat as a pin in the attire of a country gentleman, with a fine check wool coat, dark britches and gleaming top boots. In her surprise, she promptly spilled the contents of the basket all over him.

"I suppose I deserved that for giving you such a shock," he remarked, brushing small, misshapen apples off his shoulders as Miss Chatterton descended the ladder and, red-faced, loosened her skirts. She was wearing an old-fashioned dress fitted at the waist and high to the throat, washed so many times it was between blue and grey, and over it a serviceable apron with stains all down the front. Her hair was escaping from the kerchief she had tied over her head and there was a smudge on her cheek. She looked like an adorable kitchen maid.

Elliott tore his eyes from her and looked at the ground. "But," he said, looking at the misshapen apples lying there, "these are remarkably ill-favored fruit."

"Yes, the canker got into the tree before it was treated. Well, no one would probably have had it treated anyway," she confessed. "We aren't really... observant of such things. But the horses like the apples and they don't mind that they look odd, so it worked out."

"I've said it before, and I say it again, Miss Chatterton, our conversation always seems to center on the animals. It makes me wish I were a horse." He smiled at her. "But I've brought an animal who will be glad to see you, and also a newspaper from London. I thought perhaps you haven't read a recent issue."

"You've brought Horace?" cried Nina, who was trying to ignore the smile and what he had said about wishing to be a horse to capture her attention. "How kind of you! I have often wondered where he was and how he was going on. And you are right, I haven't seen the London papers, but I've had no desire to."

"You will see Horace is going on very well. He is in danger of becoming fat and lazy. He has the whole house, and me, at his beck and call."

"He is still living with you? But... but, I thought Hermione... "

"Miss Underwood has broken off her engagement with me. It was in the papers, but of course, you missed it. She found we would not suit. Horace agreed with her."

Nina's heart began to beat violently, and her head was in a whirl. Trying at the same time to push her curls up into the kerchief, she stammered incoherently, "Oh... I didn't know. I'm... please come into the house. A cup of tea? I...I should tidy myself and change my gown. Did you meet my parents?"

Lord Devin smiled at her again. "Should we first pick up the apples you were collecting for the horses? And take them to the stables? I should hate your hard work to be in vain."

"Oh, yes. Of course." She tried to collect herself. "If we leave them here the wasps will get into them."

They bent to collect the fallen apples and put them back into the basket. Once or twice, their hands almost met as they reached for the same apple. Nina drew back, as if stung. Then Elliott picked up the basket and followed her to the stables.

The horses lifted their heads as they heard her step. She visited each one, calling it by name and stroking its nose, before holding out her hand flat with an apple on it. Elliott came behind her and did the same.

"Here you are, Champion, she said, as they reached a big horse who looked vaguely familiar.

"Champion?" echoed Elliott. "Of course! This is the horse you rescued from the drayman! How fine he looks!"

"Yes, but he will never be able to hunt again or go very far. He had a very nasty hoof ulcer that took a long time to heal, and he has a spavin growth on the bone of that same leg. Poor thing, it pains him if he overdoes it. But he is a wonderful, patient animal. He is a favorite with the children on the neighboring estates, and allows them all to ride him, even the tiny ones who grab his mane and pull."

The big horse nickered on Miss Chatterton's shoulder and she put her cheek against his nose.

"He loves you, that's plain to see," said Devin. *He's not the only one*, he thought, but said nothing.

Once the apples had been distributed, Elliott accompanied Nina back across to the house. They went in through the back door, which led into the kitchens.

"Oh, I'm sorry, my lord," Nina apologized. "I come this way when I'm in my boots from the stables. I should have taken you in the front door. I didn't think."

"If I remember, on the day of our first meeting I took *you* through the kitchens, so no need to apologize," said Elliott. Though looking around him, he thought there was little comparison between the place in Devin House and what he saw here. In fact, even the stables they had just come from were in better condition than the kitchen. They had been carefully swept and newly whitewashed. The kitchens were dingy, with peeling walls and what looked like medieval cooking arrangements. Above the smoldering logs in the huge hearth hung pots and pans blackened by years of use. A large pine cupboard held rows of cracked dishes and bowls, and the long deal table in the center was covered in a variety of unwashed vegetables, including bunches of beetroot, onions, potatoes, leeks, and piles of green stuff he could not name. Amongst the vegetables there were also mud-covered boots, canes, hats and gloves.

Nina saw their visitor looking at the jumble and tried to explain. "My parents don't like to eat the flesh of animals, so our diet is mostly vegetables. The servants do occasionally eat a rabbit or pigeons. They work hard and need the meat, but we do not. And people tend to use the kitchen entrance all the time, so things get left."

Elliott shuddered and made a silent vow to find an excuse not to dine *chez* Chatterton. He very much disliked green soup. Looking at her, he made another vow to remove Nina from this environment as soon as possible. She had always been slim, but now he saw that she was skin and bone.

"Let me take you up to the drawing room, Lord Devin," she said, removing the stained apron and putting it with the collection of other items on the table, "I shall be just a few minutes changing my gown and then I look forward to renewing my acquaintance with Horace."

He nodded, thinking again she seemed to prefer the company of animals to his, and followed her up the back stairs to the front of the house. When he had arrived, the ancient butler who opened the front door had told him Miss Nina was in the orchard. He had gone straight there. He now crossed a cavernous hall and was deposited in an untidy drawing room. An old spaniel was asleep on a rug before the fireplace. He opened an eye when Nina led Elliott in, but having thumped his tail once, he closed it again and took no further notice of them.

Shapeless caps and straw bonnets with holes in them lay on top of books and pamphlets that were open over all the tables, and coats of various kinds, including more than one riding jacket and a voluminous caped cloak, had been flung over the backs of the chairs. The furniture had been good in its day, but was now stained and dilapidated; the broken leg of one of the armchairs being held up by what looked like an old wooden cartridge box. But on the walls there were some fine old oil paintings. There was a handsome fireplace, and the dimensions of the room were graceful, so that in spite of the clutter it was not unpleasant.

Left to himself, Elliott went outside to find his carriage, which his groom had driven under the shade of a massive oak. From it he lifted a basket containing a complaining Horace.

"He's been like that since you left, me lord," said the groom. "I couldn't get him to settle."

"He thinks his place is next to me," replied Elliott, "and I'm afraid I've indulged him. Take the carriage around to the stables. The horses there seem as spoiled as Horace but they may spare an apple or two for my greys."

As soon as he knew it was Elliott holding his basket, Horace quieted down and submitted to being carried inside.

"In any other house I would ask permission to let you out," said his lordship, freeing the cat, "but here I think they would be perfectly happy to see me in the basket and you out. I wonder, though, what you'll make of the spaniel."

For in London his lordship had no dogs, and though there were several at his estate in the country, they were working animals and not indoors. Horace's acquaintance with other domestic animals was consequently totally lacking. Of course, Horace did not consider himself a domestic animal of any kind. He was his master's right-hand man, and save Lord Devin himself, inferior to no one.

He now walked around the room, his tail in the air, sniffing suspiciously at the furniture legs that no doubt bore the scent of other interlopers. Suddenly, coming around the corner of the sofa, he espied the spaniel. He stopped, stiffened, arched his back and lifted one paw. Then when he saw the curious thing in front of him apparently offered no threat, he walked on tiptoe right up to it. He lightly touched the dog's nose with a curious paw. The dog opened one eye, then two. He lifted his head, and his ears swung free. Horace withdrew the paw from the nose and tapped an ear, once, twice. The spaniel, with a lifelong experience of cats, whom he thought very silly creatures and best ignored, decided this one was no more worth his time than the others. He sighed, flopped his head down and closed his eyes again.

Horace waited a few moments, padded a little closer to the warm, peaceful animal, and then lay down next to him. Obviously this was a new sort of cushion provided for his comfort. Presently, he, too, slept.

Chapter Thirty-Two

Elliott watched Horace's performance with amusement. He could see his next duty was going to be to provide a spaniel for the cat's benefit. A grandfather clock, twelve minutes fast by his lordship's pocket watch, ticked soporifically in one corner of the room. A fly droned, bumping against the sunlit windows. It was very peaceful. He felt his own eyes beginning to close.

Then a step sounded in the hall, and Nina came in. She had changed into a pale yellow dimity dress that deepened the brown of her eyes and picked out the chestnut in her curls. She had washed the smudge from her face and tied her hair back with a yellow ribbon. She looked very much the young lady of the house, though, pretty as she was, Elliott thought he preferred the dirty face and faded old dress.

"I asked Wotton to order tea," she said, "though I must confess, the servants are a little… slow."

"That will give us time to talk, then," said Elliott, "before having to perform the difficult task of holding a cup in one hand, a saucer in the other and trying to consume a piece of cake."

"Oh, I doubt there will be cake," said Nina seriously. "We may consider ourselves lucky to get a slice of bread and jam, and that's only if Wotton tells cook we have an important visitor."

"Well, I hope he didn't think me that," Elliott laughed, "so we may be saved the juggling act."

Hearing Nina's voice, Horace had awoken from his slumber and now leaped into her lap, purring like distant thunder.

"Horace!" she cried, with pleasure. "My, what a handsome fellow you are becoming! Whoever would have thought that scrawny little kitten could turn into you? Really, Lord Devin, he's a credit to you!"

"Please call me Elliott," said Devin. "You were wont to do so before, when we were all friends in London."

"Yes, but that was before… before my disgrace."

"Ah yes, your disgrace. No one who knew you believed in it. I certainly didn't. And when I confronted Mr. Smith, or Walker, as he made himself known to you, he admitted the truth."

"You met him? How? Why? It was Mr. Parsons who was behind it all, you know." Nina's face was stark as she thought of the dreadful events of that night.

"I know. I made it my business to find out. I was sure you would not willingly have done what you were accused of. You were the victim of spiteful revenge. You know, Nina, if you had explained it to Gaynor, he would have believed you."

"Believed me, perhaps," she replied in a low voice, "but unconsciously blamed me for the rest of his life. He is a good man, but too conservative to be really happy with a wife who has a stain on her character. I couldn't live like that. Besides, I… I found that I didn't want to marry him after all. I didn't love him, you see."

Elliott's heart rose. He had been afraid she had truly loved the man and had cut off the engagement because she felt she had to, not because she wanted to.

"Then I hope you will not be too hurt when I show you this."

He handed her the newspaper he had brought, folded to the Court and Society pages. Taking it from his hands, she read:

Mr. Enoch Underwood is pleased to announce the betrothal of his only daughter Hermione to Colonel Mitchell Gaynor, late of the 11th Light Dragoons. The wedding will take place in late September.

"Oh good!" said Nina. "I always thought he loved her. I knew I was his second choice."

She smiled at Elliott and he could see she was telling the truth.

"And perhaps you'd also like to see this article, which, coincidentally, appeared on the same day."

He refolded the newspaper, though not to the front page on which headline ran:

Clapped in Irons No More!
Prisoners not to be shackled in British gaols

It was reported that the Gaols Act, based on the prison reforms promoted by Elizabeth Fry and so disliked by Mr. Parsons, had now been passed by Parliament.

He turned instead to one of the inner pages, and handed it back to her. With growing astonishment, she read:

> *Users of the hackney carriages that are a constant feature of the Capital must have noticed an improvement. The carriages are cleaner, the horses healthier and the drivers less inclined to cheat their customers.*
> *Upon investigation, it appears that Mr. Albert Parsons, the owner of the company that previously ran the majority of these conveyances, has sold up and gone – we know not where.*
> *The new owner is something of a mystery. We have been unable to discover his name. The young Mr. Richard Topper, who is now running the business along enlightened principles hitherto unseen in businesses in our city, is close-mouthed about who is behind him.*
> *But to him, and to Mr. Topper, we say, thank you. Once again, we see how the character of the British, with our sense of right and justice, makes us a model for the rest of the world.*

"Good gracious!" said Nina "Mr. Parsons has gone? What can have induced him to give up his business, do you suppose? When I asked him in Christian charity to simply feed the horses a little better, he showed me the door. And who on earth can have bought it from him?"

"One can only suppose greater pressure was brought to bear on Mr. Parsons than Christian charity," replied his lordship, choosing to ignore the second question. "But it is not that I wish to draw your attention to. Don't you see, Nina? Your name is nowhere mentioned. Yet it was you who first exposed Mr. Parsons in the newspapers. If the reporters have forgotten your name, so has everyone else. Your disgrace, as you call it, is over. It was a nine-days wonder. You can return to London."

"Oh!" said Nina, doubtfully and shook her head. "I don't think…"

Well, if you still feel a little conspicuous, you can always change your name."

"Change my name?" repeated Nina in astonishment. "What on earth to?"

"To Devin, for example," answered his lordship, quietly.

It took a moment for Nina to grasp the implication of his words. "Devin?" she said, wonderingly, "you mean…"

"Yes, my dear. My mother is not proposing to adopt you, so that's exactly what I mean."

He stood up from the chair and went on one knee before her. From her lap, Horace looked at him with satisfaction.

"Wilhelmina Chatterton, will you do me…"

But before he could finish, a disheveled older gentleman of about average height came wandering into the room. His grey hair was in his eyes and his neckcloth, if that's what it was, though looking at it with a critical eye, Elliott would not have given it the name, had fallen from its folds and hung limply down the front of his misbuttoned waistcoat. He was wearing a woolen coat with great rents in the elbows. In fact, it looked in much worse condition than the coats lying over the backs of the chairs. He wore a superannuated pair of britches of a color impossible to name, and his feet were in a pair of boots that hadn't been cleaned in a twelvemonth, if not more. He was holding a bunch of some sort of leaves in his hand.

"I just found this sorrel," he said to the room in general. "I wonder if cook could make some soup with it."

"Papa," said Nina, standing up with Horace under her arm, "This is Lord Elliott Devin. He is asking me to marry him... I think. And I want to. You would approve, wouldn't you?"

"What?" The untidy gentleman was more interested in Horace. "Is that a cat?"

He peered myopically at Horace and then at Elliott, who had risen from his knee and was now looking in amusement at his future father-in-law.

"Nice looking cat! He's not ours is he? Oh, yes, you want to marry this feller. I'm sure that will be all right. Best ask your mother. Where is she, anyway?" He put the sorrel on a cluttered side table and wandered off.

"That was my father," said Nina unnecessarily. "He's a little... distracted. But he didn't seem to mind my marrying you. That *is* what you were going to ask, isn't it?"

She suddenly had the awful thought he was going to ask her something else.

"Oh! You weren't just going to ask if Horace could come and live here, were you?" She lifted dismayed eyes to his face.

"Of course not, you goose!" He laughed and caught her around the waist. "He wouldn't stay, anyway. Look, I'm damned if I'm going to kneel down again. Wilhelmina Chatterton, will you marry me?"

"Yes, yes! If you really mean it!" cried Nina. "But I'm sure you can't!"

"I most certainly do!" Elliott tried to kiss her, but was hampered by Horace who was still under her arm. He was glad to see his two favorite people together at last, but he didn't relish being squeezed between them. Struggling to free himself, he leaped from between them with a great cry. He dashed over to his friend the spaniel, who, rudely awoken by receiving a large flying cat in his side, let out a loud *woof*!

Elliott was holding Nina in his arms, and both were laughing, when suddenly a little lady of somewhat rounder proportions than Nina, but with the same determined chin and clearly her mother, entered the room. She stopped in surprise.

"Nina, my love," she said, "Your papa said there was a new cat in the drawing room and he had sorrel for soup but left it somewhere. I guessed it was here. So here I come and find you in the embrace of... who are you, exactly, young man?"

Elliott removed his arms from around Nina, bowed and said, "Elliott Devin, at your service, Ma'am. I believe I have the approval of your husband to pay my addresses to your daughter and I'm afraid we were engaging in a little premature celebration. But he did say we'd best ask you."

"I expect he did, the dear man. So, you are the Elliott Nina has talked so much about," said Mrs. Chatterton.

Nina made as if to protest, but was cut off by her Mama.

"Oh yes you have, my dear. I have never before heard you mention any man as often as Mr. Devin, even your ex-fiancé. But before I give my approval, I must hear from you, young man. You know our poor Nina left London in disgrace. We don't care. We trust our daughter and love her just the same. But that disgrace will rub off on her husband. I do not want to hear of another broken engagement. Though I never thought the Colonel was the man for her. Too stuffy, I thought, when he came here to ask for her hand, so perhaps it was all for the best. I know it is not a popular view, but I strongly believe that being married to someone you cannot love must be a lifelong torture. With my dear husband Adrian, we have always been a happy household in that regard, and I wish no less for my daughter. Now, Mr. Devin, you must give me your word that if you marry Nina you will love and stand by her even though you may be shunned by society for doing so."

"Mama! He is not *Mr.* Devin, he's *Lord* Devin," said Nina, in some embarrassment.

"I don't care if he's the Duke of Devonshire," retorted her mother with spirit, "I will not marry my daughter to a man who is ashamed of her."

"Mrs. Chatterton," replied his lordship, who had not missed the loving way his beloved's Mama talked of both her husband and her daughter, "I give you my word, I will love and cherish your daughter Wilhelmina all the days of our lives. I have every reason to believe that my standing in society is sufficient to render unimportant anything she may have done before our marriage. If it is not, and people shun her, they will have to shun me too. I care not for their opinion, I only care for her."

Nina burst into tears and threw herself onto the sofa, burying her face in one of the stained cushions. Elliot sat beside her and pulled her onto his broad shoulder, murmuring into her ear.

"Don't be silly, dear," said her mother, calmly. "It was handsomely said. Very well, *Lord* Devin, you have our permission to marry our dear girl. And talking of handsome, that is a very good-looking cat. Yours, I presume, my lord. One can always tell a happy home by the condition of the cat who lives there. You are a lucky girl, Nina. Stop crying and give your suitor a kiss. Now, where is that sorrel? I shall take it to cook for soup. You will stay for dinner, Lord Devin."

It wasn't a question, but Elliott accepted with a smile. For his Nina, he'd even eat green soup. Luckily for him, she was an obedient daughter and had turned to kiss him, as her mother had ordered. He was just taking her in his arms when the elderly butler opened the door and came in bearing a tarnished silver tray. On it was laid tea for two. And there was bread and jam.

Chapter Thirty-Three

As announced, September saw the wedding of the Colonel and Miss Hermione Underwood. They were declared the handsomest couple of the season. He was tall and distinguished in his regimentals, and she was lovely to behold in white silk with late-blooming pink roses in her hair. Her friend Nina was her bridesmaid, and though she looked insignificant beside her stately and beautiful friend, there was at least one gentleman who found her the prettiest lady in the assembly. The married couple settled into a pleasant, calm existence split between their country estate and the London home the Colonel bought for his new bride. In due course she produced the son and heir, a placid child who was the pride and joy of the family, especially his father. As she had intimated to Elliott, however, Hermione's sleep was never disturbed by her child. On the rare occasions he awoke during the night, he was immediately seen to by a nurse, and later a doting nanny.

The love Nina and Elliott had for each was evident from the moment they were seen together when Nina returned to the capital. To his friend Marius's dismay, Elliott's languid insouciance deserted him. More than once his friend arrived too late at Devin House for even a sip of that fine port. Elliott was ready to go. He wanted to arrive on time at all the places he knew his beloved would be.

Nina was so besotted she had eyes for nothing and no one but him. She forgot to comb her hair, lost her gloves, mislaid her reticule and insulted acquaintances by walking straight past them, her eyes fixed only on him. The gentle fondness the Colonel and Hermione demonstrated to each other in public was much more *comme il faut*, but when Hermione remonstrated with her friend that it was not good *ton* to wear one's heart on one's sleeve, Nina paid her not one jot of attention. Even the most starched matrons of the *ton* recognized true love, and though they expressed the obligatory criticism of Devin's behavior in flaunting a woman they all knew to be disgraced, it was done without enthusiasm. Elliott had been right. By the end of the season hardly anyone remembered anything about it, and by the next, no one did.

Miss Wilhelmina Chatterton and Lord Elliott St. John Devin were married just a month after their friends on one of the last glorious days of the year. Nina wore a gown of ivory lace bought for her by her fiancé. He didn't trust her, he said, not to show up in her stable boots and blue dimity.

"But Elliott," she declared when she saw the dressmaker's bill, "we could feed all the hackney horses for a year for less!"

"I know, my love," he replied with a sincerity belied by the twinkle in his eye, " I thought about that and decided if we face ruin after the wedding, we can sell the gown for horse fodder."

After the new dresser also arranged by his lordship gave up trying to fix a floral headdress in Nina's unruly curls, it was decided she would wear a simple veil. But even then, they made their escape. As its golden light poured through the pillars in front of St. George's Church and her veil flew behind her, the sun struck gold into the curls tumbling willy-nilly onto the bride's cheeks. Her handsome husband smiled tenderly and handed her up into a new carriage he had built specially for her. It had footrests that let down under the seats. He said he was damned if he was going to leave for his honeymoon in a carriage with his knees up to his ears, and neither was she going to ride in one where her feet didn't touch the floor. Characteristically, she said she didn't care how or where she rode, so long as it was with him.

One of the first things Nina had done on returning to London was to visit the erstwhile Parsons' stables. She could not believe the difference. Here was order and cleanliness; rows of well-built stalls housed horses that looked healthy and rested. She recognized the lad who had worked there during Parsons' time and asked him what had happened.

"Ole Parsons sold up and Dick, he come," he said simply.

And if it wasn't precisely that simple, there was no doubt that Dick was responsible for it all. Nina didn't recognize him when she saw him, and no surprise, for he had filled out and had grown whiskers. When she had seen him in Elliott's stables all those months before, he had been an overgrown boy. Now he was a man. He was still only twenty, but he had married his best girl and was father of a fat-cheeked baby who resembled him in the intelligence in his eyes and the straw-like hair that refused to lie down.

For many months, Nina didn't know of the connection between her husband and the manager of the hackney stables. Then one day, she was coming down the stairs at Devin House when she saw the top of Minton's and another man's head as they crossed to the study door and heard him say, "Dick Topper to see you, my lord."

She ran swiftly the rest of the way down the stairs and without preamble, burst into the study. She looked at the two men and suddenly understood.

"It was you, Elliott, who bought Parsons' business!"

And then something about the younger man struck her as familiar. "I remember you now! You were the one who recognized the problem with Champion's hoof!"

Elliott smiled at her. "Yes, I did, my love, and Dick here has been doing a wonderful job with it. Please join us if you'd like to hear his report."

Nina was bursting to know how it all came about, but recognized that was not the moment. She joined in the discussions and thereafter became an active participant in decisions regarding the stables, particularly, of course, the horses.

Later on as they took tea alone in the drawing room, Elliott finally confessed the whole of his involvement with Parsons and James Smith.

"I could think of no better way of punishing him than to do to him what he tried to do to you," said his lordship, his face unusually stern. "He had social aspirations. When he was dismissed in disgrace from his club, he felt it more than he would have any financial setback. He put up only a show of resistance to selling his business. Besides, you had put a hefty crimp in it with your campaign. I believe he was glad in the end to return where he came from. As for young Smith, I've no idea where he went, but he isn't in London any more. I had my solicitors check."

"I can't believe you would do all that for me!" said Nina, coming to kneel beside him, taking his hand and putting it to her cheek. Horace, who was in his usual position on his lordship's knee, wondered if he should object to having the hand that had been stroking him removed in such a way, but since he prided himself on being responsible for their union, he just continued to purr.

"I did it for Horace's sake," said Elliott. "He hates Hermione and he loves you. I had no choice in the matter." He smiled down at her and kissed the hand holding his. "I had to marry you, you must see that."

"Of course," agreed Nina.

Horace said nothing but looked very self-satisfied. And the three of them remained there, perfectly content, in front of the fire.

The End

If you enjoyed this story, please leave a review on Amazon. Reviews are REALLY important for independent authors, like me!

Please go to the book page on Amazon, scroll down and click the "review" link. Thank you!

Please go to my website up for a free short story and to listen to the first chapters of all my books:

https://romancenovelsbyglrobinson.com

You will find a link to all my other books on my author page on Amazon:

(USA) Amazon.com: GL Robinson

(UK amazon.co.uk: GL Robinson

You will find information about them all on the next few pages.

Please contact me via my website if you have any questions or comments Thank you!

The "Earl" or House of Hale series is a trilogy, though the books may be read independently.

Book One: *The Earl and The Mud-Covered Maiden*

Lysander nearly runs over Sophy in a muddy lane. Not a very auspicious beginning. But things get worse before they get better!

Book Two: The Earl and His Lady

Sophy and Lysander are happily married, but Sophy is not accustomed to life in high society and Lysander is proud of the family name. Their road to happiness is decidedly rocky.

Book Three: The Earl and The Heir

Lysander and Sophy now have Sylvester, a three-year-old son who gives them fits. Sophy adores her husband but is curious about his life before he met her. Sylvester is curious, too. Their curiosity gets them both in trouble.

In the second series the titles have the first names of the heroines.

Imogen or Love and Money.

Wealthy and beautiful young widow Imogen thinks she will find happiness investing her late husband's fortune. She does, but what then?

Cecilia or Too Tall to Love.

Orphaned Cecilia, too tall and too outspoken for acceptance by the *ton,* is determined to open a school for girls in London's East End slums, but is lacking funds. When Lord Tommy Allenby offers her a way out, will she get more than she bargained for?

Rosemary or Too Clever to Love.

Governess Rosemary is forced to move with her pupil, the romantically-minded Marianne, to live with the girl's guardian, a strict gentleman with old fashioned ideas about young women should behave. Can she save the one from her own folly and persuade the other that she isn't just a not-so-pretty face?

The latest series is "The Lord and..."

The Lord and The Red-Headed Hornet

Amelia is a fiery red-head determined to find a position for her handsome twin brother that does not involve going into the army. She talks her way into a job as the secretary to a Lord, a post usually reserved for a man. But when her brother joins the army anyway, and her employer disappears, can she save them both?

Coming in the Fall of 2021:
The Lord and The Unwilling Mistress

High class courtesan Héloise says no. His lordship is furious and can't work out why. But she isn't about to tell him the truth about her background.

And not just for Christmas but for delicious short reads any time of the year:

The Kissing Ball. A Collection of Short Stories

Please leave reviews and feel free to contact me. I love to hear from my readers

About the Author

GL Robinson was born and educated in the south of England, but has lived for over forty years in the USA with her American husband. She tried and failed to adopt an American accent, so people still call her the English Lady! She is a retired French professor, and loves flowers in the garden, eating with friends and talking with her grandchildren. She has published two children's travel books for ages 8-11 inspired by one of them.

She was inspired to start writing after the unexpected death of her dear sister in July 2018. They were educated in a convent boarding school and would giggle at Regency Romances after lights-out under the covers. All her Regency Romances are dedicated to her sister.

For more information about the author, to listen to her read from her books, receive a free short story, or get sneak previews of upcoming books, please go to:

https://romancenovelsbyglrobinson.com

Printed in Great Britain
by Amazon